T0367949

The Stage Play of
The Final Escape
In Three Acts

Other Novels

Life is Good

A Tale of Discovery

Shelter in Place

A Case of Espionage

The Terrorist Plot

The Final Escape

The Stage Play of
The Final Escape
In Three Acts

HARRY KATZAN JR.

THE STAGE PLAY OF THE FINAL ESCAPE IN THREE ACTS

iUniverse books may be ordered through booksellers or by contacting:

iUniverse
1663 Liberty Drive
Bloomington, IN 47403
www.iuniverse.com
844-349-9409

ISBN: 978-1-6632-7087-0 (sc)
ISBN: 978-1-6632-7089-4 (hc)
ISBN: 978-1-6632-7088-7 (e)

Library of Congress Control Number: 2025902421

Print information available on the last page.

iUniverse rev. date: 02/14/2025

For Margaret Now and Forever
With Love and Affection

Contents

Introduction

This is a three act play that combines a set of intelligent and dependable people engaged in a clandestant operation, that takes place, figuratively speaking of course, in the United States. Actually, the scenes are actually on the stage and the remainder of locations is inherent in the imagination of the viewer. The contents of the play are not make believe; they could actually happen and probably have. The team of Matt, Ashley, and the General are brought into the affair through no fault of their own. The play is derived from an easy to read novel entitled The Final Escape. The characters are introduced forthwith and then again as the play progresses. There are three acts that can be adjusted by the director. Moreover, the dialog can be adjusted during the familiarization process and can even be adjusted to some extent by the participants. The play is suitable for a high school, college, and an appropriate community project. It also would be be a good professional play or movie. This subject will not be mentioned again. The author scene selection in the plays will be one of the best parts of the adoption. There is one aditional fact. It is necessary that the proper actor is assigned to the various parts. Proper part selection is essential. Lastly for this introductory script, there is no sex, no bad language, and no violance in the play. The play is suitable for all readers. In the modern world, practically anything can be suggested. The play has some loose ends, and they are precisely to give the audience something to wonder and talk about afterwords. "Could this have happened here?"

Act I introduces the characters and the environment. From a design poiht of view, the character is who and what they are. There is no mention of the function they play; it developes as the drama progresses.

Act II describes the environment and the events that represent a real life situation. This act has both descriptinve and real life and overtones and circumstances. There is no violance, no sex, and no bad language. You have seen this before because it sounds good and is good. However, real life characteristions and interactive behavior lend themselves them to the world of the year 2024 and its everyday events. It represents what people do.

Act III enlarges on an interactive presentation with which the problem can be addressed. Thus events take place in the United States, London, and Iran.

This play has educational benefits in the sense there are changes between the book and the play. Students of the discipline can evaluate how things evolve and provide needed insight into the manner in which society evolves. It is a good teaching tool. Happy learning. There is a good term paper residing in the subject matter.

Harry Katzan Jr.

This volume conains two books:

The Script of
The
Final Escape
In Three Acts

The Final Escape
(A novel)

The books are organized separately.

The topics in the script are selected from the novel.

Other Novels and Plays

Life is Good

A Tale of Discovery

Shelter in Place

A Case of Espionage

The Terrorist Plot

The Play of the Money Affair

For Margaret Now and Forever
With Love and Affection

Introduction

This is a reprint in readable form of the script of the Play of Two Necessary Escapes. It is a three act play that combines a set of intelligent and dependable people engaged in a set of clandestine operations, that take place, figuratively speaking of course, in the United States, Europe, and the Middle East. Actually, the scenes are actually on the stage and the remainder of locations is inherent in the imagination of the viewer. The contents of the play are not make believe; they could actually happen and probably have. The play is derived from an easy to read novel entitled The Case of the Two Escapes. The characters are introduced forthwith and then again as the script progresses. There are three acts that can be adjusted by the director. Moreover, the dialog can additionally be adjusted during the familiarization process and can even be adjusted to some extent by the participants. In other words, the play is fungible. The play is suitable for a high school, college, and an appropriate community project. It also would be be a good professional play or movie. This subject will not be mentioned again. That is up to the producer, the director, and the characters.

The actor scene selection in the play will be one of the best parts of the adoption. There is one additional fact. It is necessary that the proper actor is assigned to the various parts. Proper part selection is essential. Lastly for this introductory script, there is no sex, no bad language, and no violence in the play. The play is suitable for all readers. In the modern world, practically anything can be imagined. The play has some loose ends, and they are precisely to give the audience something to wonder and talk about afterwords. "Could this be really happening here or maybe somewhere else?"

Act I introduces the characters and the environment. From a design point of view, the character is who and what they are. There is no mention of their function in the play; it is developed as the drama progresses.

Act II describes the environment and the events that represent a real life situation. This act has both descriptive and real life and overtones and circumstances. There is no violence, no sex, and no bad language. You have seen this before because it sounds good and is good. However, real life characterizations and interactive behavior lend themselves to the world of the year 2025 and its everyday events. It represents what people do.

Act III enlarges on an interactive presentation with which the problem can be addressed. Thus events take place in the United States and worldwide, although the implication of other areas is relatively mild.

Act IV introduces the future in which the problem domain of the current and near future exists. The play lends itself to an audience of all generations.

This play has educational benefits in the sense there are changes between the book and the play. Students of the discipline can evaluate how things evolve and provide needed insight into the manner in which society evolves. It is a good teaching tool. Happy learning. There is a good term paper residing in the subject matter. In the script, the italics items are the speaking roles of the various characters.

Characters

The characters are more important in this play than in other works in this domain. In short, what the characters do in the play is inherent in then manner they are introduced as the play progresses.

The performance centers around three people: Dr. Matt Miller, the intelligent leading character, Prof. Ashley Miller, Matt's wife, who keeps the action rolling with her wit and charm, and Dr. General Les Miller, a former outstanding military person and Matt's grandfather. All are related in one way or another.

Matt Miller, who has his PhD from a prestigious university carries the intelligence of their action. He is relatively tall, slender, and well former both physically and mentally. He is well tanned from hours on the golf course, and normally dresses like a math professor that he is.

Ashley Miller, Matt's wife, is an actress, and also professor of drama and the media. She has medium height, is beautiful looking, and wears garments and makeup like a movie actor. She wears dresses and high heeled shoes, unusual in the modern world.

Les Miller is is Matt's grandfather, called the General, is a retired general officer in the military, and is slightly shorter than Matt Miller and plays a lot of golf with him. These three characters carry carry the majority of the action scenes.

Margarite Pourgoine, the General's wife and called Anna for some unknown reason, is the General's wife and a professor of creative writing at the university. When she has something to say, which is not often, it is important.

Other characters are: **Harry Steevens**, a math friend of Matt's and a local policemen, **Kimberly Scott**, a government employee who handles data and is never seen but carries a serious voice, and lastly, **General Mark Carter**, who is a typical military general, perhaps a little overweight, and serves the nation as Director of Intelligence. Other characters are not specifically determined and should be selected by the producer and director based on the the role they play. As an example, a college student looks like a college student.

This is a modern play. There should be no overweight actors, but people with good articulation that are pleasant to look at. The clothing, in all cases, match the role they are portraying at any point in time. For example, a man should not be wearing a tux to get a haircut and a woman should not be wearing a dress and high heels to keep house.

The subject of the play is important and the choice of an actor should not distract from his role in the play.

ACT I
The Environment of People and Places

Scene One.

The characters are Lieutenant Buzz Bunday, The Commander, and Lieutenant Les Miller

The location is an airfield in an American war zone where combat airplanes land after a mission in the conflict. There should be a small building with a barrier for injured planes to run into for safety. Buzz should be wearing a pilot's uniform and the air force commander is wearing the uniform and insignia of a leader. Buzz is agitated because his buddy Lieutenant Miller has not returned. There is sound of flight action in the background. This is the typical method for introducing military characters.

Lieutenant Bunday: *He should be back here by now. He chased an enemy fighter plane that shot down a U.S. B-17 bomber. I told him to forget the enemy because of the amount of fuel remaining in his P-51. I got tired of waiting for him and returned here to the base to wait for him.*

Commander: *Either he has been shot down or run out of fuel. You have got 10 minutes Lieutenant. I have work to do.*

Lieutenant Bunday: *I think I hear a P- 51. His engine doesn't sound so good.*

Commander: *His engine has just cut out and he will have to make a dead stick landing.*

The sound of a P-51 running into the barrier is heard. Lieutenant Miller jumps out of his cockpit.

Lieutenant Miller: *I got him. That's 35 kills for me.*

Commander: You *both have completed your requirement of 25 missions. Report to my office at 0800 hours tomorrow.*

The Commander leaves.

Lieutenant Bunday: *That 35 gets you an air combat medal. Congratulations buddy.*

Lieutenant Miller: *Congratulations to you also. I couldn't have gotten 35 kills without you as my wing man. Maybe, you will get a medal too. I think we are the best team in the U.S. Air Force.*

END OF SCENE ONE
ACT I

Scene Two.

The characters are Lieutenant Buzz Bunday, The Commander, and Lieutenant Les Miller.

The location is the sparsely decorated Commander's military office with a door, a desk, and a file cabinet The Commander is sitting with a cup of joe and the two Lieutenants enter by the door and salute. The Commander stands up.

Commander: *At ease Lieutenants. You have completed your flight requirement and are hereby promoted to Captain, with all of the rights and privileges pertaining thereto. The Sargent will pin your Captain's bars before you leave. You will also receive Air Combat medals and Activity Bars for your dress uniform. You have two weeks leave and then report to the Pentagon for your next assignment. You will get the medals and bars in the Pentagon. Your expenses are covered by the Government. Congratulations. Captain Bunday, your English promotion is the same. Dismissed, and lots of luck. It was a pleasure working with you. One more thing. We have a transport leaving at 1300 hours that will get you directly to the states. What you do when you get there is your business, but enjoy yourself. You are the best team I have commanded in my 10 years in the military.*

There is a brief moment of eerie silence.

Captain Miller: *You are our best Commander, as well. We couldn't done it with your knowledge and guidance. Thank you.*

This is the end of combat for the two pilots. They both shake the hand of the Commander, and hesitantly leave the office.

END OF SCENE TWO
ACT I

Scene Three.

The characters are Captain Les Miller and Captain Buzz Bunday on leave in New York City.

They are walking down 1st Avenue with the Statue of Liberty on one side and the Empire State Building kind of on the other side. They are looking at the girls and talking about how nice the United States is. The men stop and are discussing New York and the Statue of Liberty. Two very pretty girls pass. The men turn around to look at them, as men sometimes do. The girls know they are being looked at by military officers and are more than proud. They don't say a word, but stop for a few seconds.

Captain Buzz Bunday: *I am amazed by the quality of life in America. The food is so good and girls are beyond belief. Is the whole country like this? I should move here.*

Captain Les Miller: *It's even better Buzz. It gets better as we walk around in upper Manhattan. That's where the real slick girls are. There are even dance halls. It's too bad about our destination of Washington DC and the Pentagon. I wonder what is going on. I think we are more important than we think. I guess the big shots finally realized that they don't know everything. I have to say that flying in combat is quite an experience. I glad we are finished with it. Twenty five missions is quite a load; I'm really tired - down deep in my soul.*

Captain Buzz Bunday: *I feel unusually tired too. I'm really glad we are finished with aircraft combat and hope they don't* *change their mind. Do you have any idea of what we will be doing?*

Captain Les Miller: *By the way they are handling us, I think it is top secret. But who knows; everything is top secret these days.*

Captain Buzz Bunday: *Like when you ask where the bathroom is. You might get the answer, "Why do you want to know?" That would be a good place to hide something.*

Captain Les Miller: *I wish this war were over. Everything is rationed: gas, food, sugar, butter – oh that's food. They collect tin foil from candy bars, if you can find one. Also, nylon stockings to give to women in the war zone. They didn't even wear them before the war. You can't buy a car. You can't find cigarettes and have to resort to that roll-your-own brand. People all over are buying $25 war bonds to help with the cost of the war. You pay $18.75 for them and they are worth $25 when they mature. Even the automobile workers are being used in the factories to make bomber planes and fighter planes. There is one place, I think in Cleveland, where they can turn out 16 bombers in one day. They even have women working. I've heard they are good. They have a name but I can't remember it.*

Captain Buzz Bunday: *Where do you hear about all this stuff?*

Captain Les Miller: *Letters from home, and they even sensor them. If your script is bad enough, the sensors can't read them, and they pass them through. They think that if they can't read them, the enemy can't either.*

Harry Katzan Jr.

Captain Buzz Bunday: *Wow. Holy smoke. Look at those two nice looking chicks. They are heading right to us. They look interested.*

Captain Les Miller: *They are looking at us. It's too bad we have to go the Washington tomorrow. I think the train leaves at 6:30 AM. We had better hit the hay. No girls for us.*

This is the end of New York and the girls for the two P-51 pilots, who are now Captains.

END OF SCENE THREE
ACT I

Scene Four.

The characters are military officers in dress uniforms, scientists, Professors, the Commander and newly promoted Captains Miller and Bunday.

The scene is a conference room in the Pentagon. There are slogans all over the walls. The chairs are arranged in a in complicated form of disarray. There are officers, scientists, professors, and math people sitting around in some random form and there is a table at which the Commander will be sitting. The military men are dressed smartly in their dress uniforms and the remainder aren't in any particular form of dress. It would appear that the men who have the most to say are dressed the worst. They all act like like they are the world's smartest people. Yet they have not been able to solve the problem of the high number of P-51s that have been shot down. They have tried amour plating and it hasn't worked. This problem has been going on for some time and the men are frustrated. The wall has a substantial door. Then the Commander comes in with Captain Les Miller and Captain Buzz Bunday. The men in the room are talking like they own the world but quiet down when the Commander comes in. The non-military characters are any old form of man. The precise number of men is not established.

Commander: *Attention gentlemen. I would like to introduce Captain Miller and Captain Bunday. They are back from the war zone. They are to be congratulated. They will receive Air Combat medals and Activity Bars.*

A military aid pins the Air Combat medals and Activity bars onto the uniforms of Captain Miller and Captain Bunday.

The audience claps, but rather weakly. Captain Miller and Captain Bunday have big smiles on their faces. They are proud.

Commander: *They are here to assist us with the problem that too many P-51s are being shot down in ordinary bombing missions. We, as a strategic force in the war, cannot sustain the fact that a high failure rate of 90% of the P-51 aircraft cannot be sustained in terms of personnel and aircraft.*

The Commander displays P-51 photographs showing various angles of the aircraft that have returned.

Commander: *We have tried to armor plate the planes with titanium and it didn't seem to make a difference. We have selected all clean areas on the aircraft for armor plating.*

Captain Miller: *I can solve your problem gentlemen, and reduce the failure rate to roughly 10% which I can imagine would be satisfactory.*

A scientist stands up.

Scientist: *The Captain is off his rocker. There are professors, scientists, and Generals here that can't solve the problem and a recently promoted Captain says he can solve the problem. He is totally crazy.*

All of the men in the room just laugh.

Commander: *Let's take a coffee break gentlemen and take up the problem again in 10 minutes.*

Captain *Les* Bunday: *Are you out of your mind? You are going to get us demoted on our first day as Captains.*

Captain Miller: *Don't worry Buzz. I'll take care of it.*

Captain Bunday: *What did you major in at college?*

Captain Miller: *Math. Don't worry about it.*

 END OF SCENE FOUR
ACT I

Scene Five.

The characters are The same as scene four.

The other men come back into the room and take their seats. Most of them are laughing. Some just look dejected.

Captain Bunday. *I hope you are right buddy.*

Commander: *Did you want to continue Captain Miller?*

Captain Miller stands up.

Captain Miller: *Thank you. The objective of this meeting is to determine where titanium plates should be placed for protection of the P-51s with bullet hole damage. Here some photos.*

Captain Miller holds up some photos.

Captain Miler: *The photos show P-51s with bullet holes. The planes have been plated where the holes are with no improvement. That's the reason we are here. It's an easy problem.*

The rest of the audience just laughs. Another officer speaks:

An Officer: *The guy is an idiot. I thought the reason they are here is to help us. The new Captain is totally off his rocker. This is a tough and important problem, and we need to solve it as quickly as possible.*

Captain Miller calmly continues.

Captain Miller: *It's easy gentlemen. The important holes went down with the plane – in fact – probably caused it. Look at the photos, do you see any planes with holes in their bellies. We should be plating areas where there are no holes.* I repeat, places with no holes. They bring down the aircraft.

The audience in the room just looked at each other. That was the solution to their problem.

Captain Miller continues. No one says a word.

Captain Miller: *If the Army Air Force would armor plate the untouched areas, evident in the photos that we have, then the problem will be solved. For identification, we can call the operation 'Reverse Mathematics.'*

END OF SCENE FIVE
ACT I

Scene Six.

The characters are The same as scene four.

This scene is subsequent to scene five. Some time has passed. The members of the group file back into the military room. The same room as scene five, but the organization is different reflecting a later time period. The commander takes the stage, so to speak.

The Commander: *This will be a short meeting, gentlemen. We all have work to do, and I know your time is limited. I am pleased to announce that Captain Miller's solution named reverse mathematics has reduced the problem. The amour placed in clean aircraft bellies and the percentage of shot down P-51s was reduced to 10%.*

The audience just looked at the two Captains with pleasure, and some of them offered a handshake.

The Commander: *Captions Miller and Bunday. Attention! You are now promoted to the rank of Major in the Army Air Force with all the privileges pertaining thereto. This is a bit unusual, but we are all operating in unusual times. The number of saved men and aircraft was quite large, and it noticeably changed the nature of the combat operation. Congratulations.*

END OF SCENE SIX
ACT I

Insert for the reader:

This is a true story. The author has researched the subject and read the descriptive math paper that describes it. It was termed reverse mathematics here for lack of a better name. A distinguished professor eventually worked on it for some time and named it survivorship bias.

Reference:

Ellenberg, J., How not to be Wrong. New York: Penguin Press, 2014, p. 3-9.

Scene Seven.

The characters in this scene are Les Miller, now a Colonel in the Army Air Force, a driver that is a Sargent called Bud in the Army Air Force, and a beautiful young woman whose light military vehicle has run off the road in rural England. The U.S. jeep is on the audience left and pointing in that direction. The truck is at an angle off the road and the woman is standing at the edge of the muddy road. She is located at the audience right, about 20 feet from the men. She is wearing a British female military uniform.

Miller's job is to check returning P-51 flights and perform an assessment of damage imposed by the enemy. Then based on necessary analytics, initiate protective measures available from aircraft vendors. Then, go to their next air base and do the same thing. The travel between bases is treacherous, and it is often necessary to eat K rations and sleep in a pup tent. The K rations are good and include a chocolate bar and a pack of Lucky Strike cigarettes. The officers also have nylon stockings to give to the local residents, even though they probably did not have them beforehand. The relationship between U.S. military men and English folk is quite good.

Miller driven by Bud pass the women for security reasons and then back up to offer assistance. She is a Second Subattern, I.e. a second lieutenant, in the women's auxiliary corps.

Colonel Miller: *Are you okay?*

The Woman: *I'm just a bit frightened. I've been off the road for a long while, and thought that no one would show up to assist me. You are Americans?*

Colonel Miller: *We are both Americans. Let us help you.*

The jeep, a remarkable little vehicle, pulls her out of the mud and the conversation continues.

Colonel Miller: *We are traveling between cases; we work on airplanes.*

The Woman: *You are a Colonel. Do you fly airplanes? My name is Mary Wales, by then way.*

Colonel Miller: *I am a pilot. My name is Les Miller and my driver is Sergeant Bud Small. By the way, would you like some chocolate, or cigarettes, or nylons. We have chocolate and cigarettes from our K rations, and they give us nylons to give to women we encounter. We know that some times are not available in England.*

Mary Wales: *I would appreciate some chocolate and nylons. I am very hungry and have been waiting here, off the read, for a long time.*

Bud Small: *Are you sure you don't want cigarettes?*

Mary Wales: *No thank you. I don't smoke. Smoking is bad for you.*

Bud Small: *That's probably true. Some people don't care. We don't smoke either. That's why we have them to give away.*

Colonel Miller: *You are very brave. Most women don't want to help out with the war effort. You look like my sister. She is very beautiful.*

Mary Wales: *Thanks for the complement. Can I give you a good old British hug?*

Colonel Miller: *Sure, and I'll give you an American hug in return.*

Mary Wales and Colonel Miller give each other a hug.

Mary Wales hesitates. *Miller wonders why. He looks up.*

Mary Wales: *This is the first hug I have ever been given. People don't touch me.*

The remark is left unanswered and the two vehicles proceed in opposite directions.

Colonel Miller: *Nice looking girl. I hope she makes it wherever she is going.*

Bud Small: *You bet.*

ENDS OF SCENE SEVEN
ACT I

Scene Eight.

The characters are Matthew Miller, usually referred to as Matt and Ashley Wilson are both students. A Professor named Marguerite Purgoine, known as Anna is also in the scene. There are also students seated in a medium sized room, lined with books.

The scene is a stairway on the left, an open door, and a small classroom filled with students looking outward. Two seats are free. The two students, Matt and Ashley, are trudging up. The young man - i.e., Matt begins the conversation.

Matt: *Hi, my name is Matthew Miller, but most people call me Matt. Are you going to make it?*

Ashley: *Well, I think so. I'm not so Athletic, my Mom wanted to be a soccer mom, and now I hate running and exercise of all kinds. My name is Ashley Wilson.*

The couple plough upward until they reach the apartment. The door is open wide to a large studio with bookshelves and thousands of books scattered practically everywhere. The professor is standing just inside the door, and lets them in. Then professor is a small woman with gray hair and the softest skin on this side of the Mississippi. She is called Anna. The floor is flat the a stairway is simulated by the students actions.

Anna: *Welcome to creative writing.*

The couple grab the two remaining seats. Comment: This is a bit hard to envision, but it can be done. The audience is busy looking at the young students, anyway.

Anna continues: *You are in the most worthwhile course that you are going to take at this prestigious university. My name is Marguerite Purgoine and I will be your teacher. In the class and and with email and messaging, I would prefer that you call me Anna – heaven only knows where that name came from. On the street and in the university, please call me Professor Purgoine or Dr. Purgoine. I am well aware of grade inflation throughout the country and especially this campus. So just do your job and I will take care of you.*

Matt and Ashley smile at one another. Matt and Ashley become close friends and eventually get married.

Matt and Ashley turn out to be major characters in the play. In this scene, they are dressed as students.

END OF SCENE EIGHT
ACT I

Scene Nine.

The characters are Les Miller, Army Air Force Three Star General Officer, obtained through outstanding military achievement, former Three Star General and Nuremberg War Trial lawyer Bill Donovan, and two Iranian graduate students. (Just mentioned.)

In spite of an enormous contribution to the U.S. Army Air Force, General Miller encountered a major problem. The number of enteral officers is governed by congress. No slots were available for General Miller to be promoted to a Four Star General until someone retired. There is a time limit. If a slot is not available in that time limit, then then he must retire. There are ways to extend the time limit. This is the Army way. Further education is one method for extending the time limit, and Miller used it wisely.

At first, Miller contacts Donovan about the problem and a possible alternative. It starts with a telephone call between the two officers.

General Miller: *That's the problem Bill. It looks like I will have to retire. I don't see a solution for me to get my fourth star. This is peace time and things are tight. I've done some really speculative things in my career, like save a plane load of general officers and work with you on the Nuremberg trials. Someone owes me something; that's what I think, anyway.*

Donovan: *I know where you are going with this Les. It happened with me also. I took the retirement as a 3-star and got a law background. Actually, I had the Army support my law training. I'm a JD. That ended, and now I am the President* *of a university in Brooklyn, and we have a new Computer Science program. You can get a Master of Science degree in CS in a year. By then, something may open up while you are in school. If not, maybe you can add another school to the list. We have the best master's program in the world. One of the faculty wrote a bunch of books, and that served to kick our program off. I even got them a new computer. There is money all over the place. Especially in politics.*

General Miller: *I think I will go with that Bill. Perhaps I can use that knowledge to build a new business or something when I really do retire. I also wanted to get flight certified on the B-29.*

Quick change to scene ten. Lights off and then lights on. It's a way to emulate "a few years later', actually only one.

END OF SCENE NINE
ACT I

Scene Ten.

The characters are Les Miller, Army Air Force Three Star General Officer, obtained through outstanding military achievement, former Three Star General and Nuremburg War Trial lawyer Bill Donovan, and two Iranian graduate students.

This is a telephone conversation between General Miller and Bill Donovan, President of the University. Miller is about to finish his Master of Science program, and has been accepted in a PhD program, along with a slot in the B-29 training program. He is still waiting for a slot open in the Four Start General rank, and his advisor has pulled a few strings to keep Miller in the system. A few years ago, Miller had saved a plane load of General officers and apparently that meant a lot. Actually, Donovan pulled the strings and he is not letting Miller know that.

General Miller: *Hello, Bill. This is Les.*

Donovan: *Hi Les. I know it is you; it's on my phone. Modern technology is wonderful. Congratulations. I heard of your success. I have some news that you haven't heard of yet. They are holding the B-29 course during your summer vacation in that PhD program. They have divided it into two sections.*

General Miller: *It's the best we can do. If the slow doesn't open up in that time, I guess that I am going to bail out. Those Iranian students named Robert Peterson and John Evans want to get into a PhD program in math at Cal Tech. Can you help them?*

Donovan: *I have already. They do not know it yet. Just tell them who you are. They will be your friend for years. I gotta go, Les. We have a big campus meeting and I am the person running the show. Tell them they are in at Cal Tech, and you can juice it up a little by telling them you had something to do with it. Over and* out.

The Iran students are graduate assistants, and have an office of their own. Les Miller walks over to their office and tells them the result. They are overjoyed and invite Miller out to dinner. Then Miller tells them that he is an active military General and they are totally surprised.

END OF SCENE TEN
END OF ACT ONE

Harry Katzan Jr.

ACT II
A Problem is Determined

Scene One.

The characters are Matt and the General.

The characters have settled in to their respective routines. Dr. Matthew Miller is established himself as a first-rate mathematician, The General has earned his masters and doctorate degrees and has been certified as a B-29 pilot, He has been successful in business and is settled in as a person that enjoys helping people. Buzz Bunday is active in England as a member of the British Secret Service (BSS), Ashley is married to a member of British Society, but they have gone their separate ways. The General is Matt's grandfather, but are generally regarded as associates.

The general has called Matt on the telephone. The stage is dark with the two two lighted telephones at either end. The scene has already been set.

The General: *Matt, something has come up. Can we meet for dinner? I know you will say yes. How about tonight at 6:00 in the Green Room? I'll get us a private booth at the rear of the dining room.*

Matt: *It must be serious. You couldn't A tell me what it is about., could you?*

The General: *Nope.*

Matt: *I'll be there.*

The lights flick off for a few seconds, and then the lights are turned on with the stage set. The General is seated at a private booth. Matt arrives and sits down at the table in the booth. The stage was set before the previous phone conversation.

The General: *What are you having?*

Matt: *That new non-alcoholic beer called Zero. What are you drinking?*

The General: *Scotch. You are a big drinker.*

The waiter is waiting.

The General: *Scotch on the rocks and a Zero. We will order in a few minutes.*

Matt: *I don't have anything against drinking alcoholic beverages. I just never got started. It was also that way in college.*

The General: *Have you heard of the new computer database methodology called Blockchain?*

Matt: *I didn't know you were up to date on that stuff. Of course, I know about it.*

The general: *I never told you about computers and me. It is one of those things I never talked about. I have a Master of Science in Computer Science from Pratt Institute in Brooklyn. The institute has since decided to concentrate on art and design.*

Matt: *How in the world did you end up there?*

The General: *One of my former associates at OSS is the President there. He said they had a new Master of Science degree there, first in the world, and I enrolled there. And got the MS. I have a sad story about Gary Powers who was a military pilot and involved with the the President. He was flying for a California TV station. The chopper had a faulty fuel gauge that contained a nominal amount of fuel when the gauge read empty... Someone fixed the fuel gauge, so Powers thought there was fuel in the tank when it really empty. He crashed and died. That was an unfortunate case. I used my knowledge of computer knowledge to start up my political polling business. This happened when I was in the military waiting for a promotion. I also got a PhD in international relations from Princeton, all when I was waiting for a promotion from Lieutenant General, that is 3-star, to a General, that is 4 star.*

Matt looked at the General straight in the eye.

Matt: *That is some story. But I know you are stalling for some reason. What is it?*

END OF SCENE ONE.
Act II

Scene Two.

The characters are Matt and the General.

The previous scene is kept the same.

The General: *Well, it is important and it might involve your friend Ashley.*

Matt: *What has she done? Maybe I should ask if she is okay.*

The General: *Well, she is okay, and the situation doesn't involve her directly. I think. Have you heard from her?*

Matt: *Yes. She messaged me yesterday. She's in London and wants to re-marry that Prince Michael to whom she was previously married. She wants to come back to the states where he could be a Professor. He has since received his PhD from Oxford. It's not clear whether or not he knows about this. I replied with almost nothing, but I humored her to the best of my knowledge. And that's it.*

The General: *Here's the story. I received a satellite call from my old Army buddy Buzz Bunday. The Royal Family, as least the Queen and Prince Michael, know about someone known as the General who is good at solving problems of a complicated nature. However, the BSS, as a group, does not specifically know about the interest by the Queen in complicated problems, and also about me. The Queens needs someone to solve a major problem and probably some minor problems. This is another situation that could have been prevented. The record keeping in the Monarchy is poor and any checks and balances that would normally occur do not exist. That's it.*

Matt: *I think your want me to go there, and you want me to accompany you - perhaps to solve the record keeping problem.*

The General: *That's what I had in mind. Perhaps, I could solve the major problem, and you could could take care of the other one.*

Matt didn't say a word. He didn't like minor problems and the General was no ace in solving major problems. He just sat there thinking what to say.

Matt: *How long?*

The General: Probably fourteen days; maybe fifteen, but definitely not less than ten. We could take the Gulfstream and land at London City Airport. We would have to give our real names, but there doesn't appear to be a downside to that.

Matt*: Okay, just give me time to pack.*

The General: *I'll call Buzz, but there is one more sensitive thing I have to tell you.*

Matt: *I hope I'm not too surprised.*

The General: *It's another kind of surprise. You're not the only doctor in this room.*

Matt looked around.

The General: *It's me. I received a PhD in international relations from Princeton. I got it right after I passed the B-29* *pilot certification. I'm on my way to obtain a general officer upgrade.*

Matt: *Well, I'll be. You have a bachelors, masters, and doctorate. Do you have any other more surprises?*

The General: *Let's eat. We've already done a lot of work.*

Matt just looks at him.

END OF SCENE TWO
Act II

Scene Three.

Characters: The characters are Matt, the General and Buzz Bunday, the former wing man to the General. The Queen and Prince Michael are referred to.

Same setting as scene two.

The General is returning Buzz's call.

The General: *What are you doing these days, Buzz? How in the devil did you get involved with the crown, or should I say the Queen?*

Buzz: *I'm retired and enjoying life. The connection to the Queen is through my son, who is part of the BSS, and my son's connection is through Prince Michael, who is doing diplomatic service in the BSS. They only contacted me to see if I knew who the General is. I have not responded as yet, so here is my question, "Should I tell them who are and endeavor to establish a link between you and the Queen? If so, how do you want me to make the connection?"*

The General: *Just tell them who we are and tell us when to get there. My team will be Dr. Les Miller, former a General in the U.S. Army Air Force, and Dr. Matthew Miller, mathematics professor. We can give the United Kingdom 14 days of consulting time, plus or minus a day, and there will be no consulting fee or other business expenses.*

Buzz: *What is this Dr. Les Miller? I haven't heard of that.*

The General: *I earned it after I finished my B-29 pilot certification.*

Buzz: Okay buddy. I'll let you know where and when.

Matt and the General sit there looking at Matt's new satellite phone. Buzz returns the call.

Buzz: *She will expect you at the palace gate at 9:00 AM three days from now. I can arrange for transportation from London City Airport and support your needs while you are there. I have some power around the BSS.*

The General: *That was a fast response, Buzz. It must be an important problem.*

Buzz: *The Queen thinks it is. I don't have a clue as to what it is all about.*

The General: We will be arriving at the London City Airport in the Gulfstream. I'll let you know the details. Thanks, Buddy.

Buzz: *A pleasure, Buddy.*

The General tells Matt the details.

The General: We will arrive at the London City Airport on Wednesday in the afternoon, and sleep on the plane. We will need transportation to the palace at approximately 8:30 AM on Thursday. All other arrangements will be left as open items to be addressed after meeting with then Queen.

END OF SCENE THREE.
Act II

Scene Four.

The characters are the General, Matt, the Queen. The Queen is dressed in a bright green dress with suitable jewelry. Then men are dressed in black suits, white shirts, and black ties.

With the curtain closed, a pair of elves is holding the following sign with a green border to the audience:

Her Royal Highness the Queen
Announces the Following Visitors
To the Royal Monarchy

General Leslie Miller, PhD
United States Army Air Force

Professor Matthew Miller, PhD
Distinguished Mathematician

The team will be assisting the Royal Family
In the operation of The Royal Kingdom

They are a distinct honor to The Royal Family

The curtain opens to a distinguished royal meeting room. The Queen is seated, and rises when the General and Matt are escorted in to the meeting room. They offer a bow and it is waved off by the Queen. The Queen is very sophisticated and comfortable with her position as leader of the Monarchy.

The General looks at the Queen, and the Queen look at the General. They say at the same exact time:

The Queen and the General: *Do I know you?*

The Queen and the General give each other a big American hug and the Queen says:

The Queen: *I can still taste that chocolate bar that you gave me on that forlorn road during the war. I was so hungry. I saved the nylons that you gave me and I still have them.*

The General: *When I saw you on that lonely road, I thought you were the prettiest girl I had ever seen. I still do.*

Matt looks at the two of them with awe.

The Queen and the General discuss their lives.

The Queen: *My father was the King and I took over when he died. I am very busy with approximately 300 appearances in a year. One of the characteristics of being Royalty is that no one is allowed to touch you. You were the first person that has done so when we met on that lonely road. No person has touched me after that meeting on the muddy road.*

The General: *I have also been busy with being a pilot and an Army officer. Being an Army officer is a bumpy road, but I will not abstain from giving you an occasional American hug — but not in public.*

The Queen and the General move on to the current problem facing the Royal Monarchy. And the reason for their meeting.

The Queen: *We have a terrible financial problem. Someone, we know not who, has been transferring funds from several royal accounts. We don't know who that is because there are ample funds for every Royal's needs and desires. We found out about the situation from the Royal Auditor who noticed that the receiver of the transferred funds was the same numbered account. We initiated a search for the person requesting the bank transfers and it turned out to be my daughter, Princess Amelia. The Royal Auditor asked her about the bank transfers, and she indicated that it must be a mistake. She said that she had ordered none of them. There is an element of trust among royalty in that one person does not question another's integrity. I do not to bring in the police or security services since they have tendency to entertain the media with just about everything, resulting in a royal scandal. We would like to We should like to avoid a major scandal for any reason.*

The General: *What are the amounts of the bank transfers and how often do they occur?*

The Queen: *I can get that information for you. I also have the numbered account number right here.*

The General: *Do you have a general record of all financial transactions that occur — something like a ledger?*

The Queen: *We don't have anything like that. We pay no taxes, have no driving licenses, and require no identification of any sort, such as a passport. We have no need to save information.*

The General: *It is remarkable that you have a closed society, as you have in the Royalty, but in this case, it is* *counter-productive. That is precisely why we have Dr. Matt Miller with us. There are methods for keeping track of any such incidents, and Matt can set it up for you.*

The Queen: *Well, okay then. I suppose we need something like that.*

The General: *We can and will take care of both problems. I will need access to your Royal Auditor. Matt will take care of the operational situation. I can guarantee to you that we will be practically transparent. Matt will need access to the auditor and your data processing people. I think we can wrap this up in a week or 10 days.*

The queen was pleased. Matt was impressed with the situation.

END OF SCENE FOUR
Act II

Scene Five.

The characters are the Queen, the General, and Matt, plus an entourage of English royalty at the royal dinner table.

The scenes are the Royal dining room on a bright sunny Sunday; the Queen's suite on a miserable weather Monday; a pleasant day on Tuesday; and a trip home for a few round of golf on Wednesday.

The General returned from Zurich with the financial problem solved, and the Queen requested that the General and Matt accompany her to church on Sunday followed by the royal family dinner in the palace. The scene is the royal dinner table without verbal communication. It is intended to be entertaining. Displaying English customs.

The seating is carefully prepared as is the dinner. The General sits on the right of the Queen and Matt on her left. The person on the right occupies the preferred seat. The scene opens with the royal family around the table in pleasant conversation. The meal of soup, fish, roast beef, and treacle pudding is served and eaten. There is no conversation, but an unusual demonstration of the group having a pleasant meal. No work is performed on Sunday. This is not a normal scene, but establishes the power of the royalty

END OF SCENE FIVE
Act II

Scene Six.

The characters are the Queen and the General.

The General enters the Queen's suite and attempts to bow. The Queen waves him off, as usual.

The General: *Your financial problem has been solved through associates in private banking in Zürich Switzerland. We have identified the royal person involved ...*

The Queen interrupts the General.

The Queen: *I am pleased to announce that Princess Amelia has been assigned to the position of Royal Deputy to the British Ambassador in Australia. She left by private plane on Saturday night after the events in Switzerland. Since I run this operation out of London and have supreme power, I made a quick decision. There will be no more surprise expenditures under my watch.*

The General: *Do you mean that you knew that Princess Amelia was the source of the problem all along?*

The Queen*: No, I did not., but I had my suspicions. The death of her husband and your computer results in Zürich confirmed everything. You must remember that in the system of British Royalty, the Monarch is the supreme leader.*

The General: *I am surprised but pleased at your success.*

The Queen: *And now, one more thing. Would take me on a date tomorrow? I know this is common among Americans, but not for Royalty.*

The General: *I would enjoy doing that. Would you like me to make a plan for the day?*

The Queen: *I would be pleased if you did so.*

The General: *I do have one more item for your knowledge and approval. Matt has totally redone your accounting operation using a new method named Block Chain in which all operational details is recorded for your safety and approval. Your staff loves it and you can rest in total satisfaction.*

The Queen: *I will award him a special Royalty medal and a case to display it. He can display it in his university office of he so desires. In case you are wondering, you will receive one as well. Many thanks from the Monarchy team.*

End of Scene Six
Act II

Scene Seven.

The characters are the Queen and the General.

The scenes are the royal limousine, Harrods, Ritz Hotel, Simpson's on the Strand, and the royal limousine.

Mini scenes depict the activities of the Queen and the General at the various venues. (May be comical. Director's alternative.). This scene may be optional.

Mini scene #1. The Queen and the General in the plain limousine.

Mini scene #2. The Queen and the General at Harrods, and a little gift. (Black ball pen.)

Mini Scene #3. The Queen and the General at Ritz Hotel having a drink.

Mini Scene #4. The Queen and the General at Simpson's on the Strand.

Mini Scene #5. The Queen and the General in the plain limousine.

Mini Scene #6. The Queen giving the General a sophisticated kiss.

END OF SCENE SEVEN
ACT II

Scene Eight.

The characters are the General and Matt.

Matt and the General are on the return flight. Both are looking forward to a few pleasureful rounds of golf. Also, a special dinner at the Green Room was something they both looked forward to, along with their wives. Matt was in good spirits.

Matt: *I never asked, but how much do we get for this job. I worked the total night with that ancient accounting system. The existing system was a copy from the Stone Age. They are up to date now and should be okay for quite a long while.*

The General: It was gratis. I forgot to tell you. Sorry.

Matt: *No wonder we got medals. You just liked the Queen.*

The General: *I made that commitment to Buzz before we left for London. Are you going to display your medal and its case in your office?*

Matt: *Do you mean at home or at the university?*

The General: *I was thinking of the university.*

Matt: *I suppose it will be the university. At home it would have to compete with the golfing trophies in the closet. Just joking.*

The General: *I think we should up our golf dates from 2 per week to 3 per week. We can work it out. I don't know about you, but I feel I am getting a little rusty.*

Matt: *Your scores are good, so I don't feel you are actually rusty. Are you feeling rusty or just bored with the same old course? Maybe you should switch to bocce, croquet, or pickleball. They are popular these days. Then there is always fishing. Or swimming.*

Matt had a grin on his face.

Matt: *Then there is always girls. The Queen really liked you. There are a lot of 40+ ads these days.*

The General: *That's not funny. I was just being professional. She's a grand dame, and you know it.*

Matt: *I know that, and that you were just being accommodating. You are very nice about things like that. I need a nap.*

Both the General and Matt take a short nap. They had worked hard and deserved it.

END OF SCENE EIGHT
Act II

Scene Nine.

The characters are still Matt and the General.

As the scene open, they are both asleep in their seats. Nothing has changed from the previous scene. The General's satellite phone rings and he answers it. He listens for about 5 minutes and hangs up.

The General: *That was Director Clark. There is a national emergency. They have been tracking us. Since we are about 4 minutes and 30 second outside of the New Jersey Airport, they decided to send a Presidential plane to the airport. When we land, we should go directly to that aircraft. It will be running and waiting. They will take care of luggage. We will have an emergency flight to Dulles, and a Marine One chopper will have its blades moving for our trip to the White House. No information is available on this operation. We will be briefed in the President's Office. This is* TOP SECRET.

END OF SCENE NINE
ACT II

Scene Ten.

The characters are the General, Matt, Director Mark Clark, the President, The President's special assistant George Benson, also with additional characters such as airline pilots (the Airplane Captain), and other White House personnel.

Back in the Washington area, Air Force One, the President's jet plane was being readied for a fast unplanned trip. The President and Vice President were being readied for a quick trip. Having both the President and Vice President on the same flight was against regulations, but the President overruled them. This was slightly before Matt and the General had finished their work in London. The Presidential staff on the flight were minimal. The purpose of the flight and ensuing events are covered later.

This scene starts here. Matt and the General hurry off of the Gulfstream and hurry to the Presidential jet. The engines are running.

The General: *What took you so long?*

The Airplane Captain: *We are just slow people General. Good morning.*

The General: *I suspect that you don't know what is going on.*

The Airplane Captain: *Not a word. Jump in; we're late.*

The flight to DC is smooth and fast. Air traffic had been averted for their flight, reflected in their flight plan, so the trip was as fast as they could possibly make it. Marine One is waiting with its rotors running. They land in the White House heliport and in 5 minutes they are in the President's private office.

Director Clark, former General and Chief of Staff, and President Kenneth Strong are there, having tracked their flight to DC.

This is a *dynamic scene* in which the stage adjusts from the Seats in the Gulfstream to the Presidential jet, to the helicopter, to the White House and the President's private office. Essentially the scene follows Matt and the General, who sit down. It appears that Matt and the General are moving, but the stage scenery is actual moving. This is original. Director Clark starts the dialogue.

Director Clark: *Mr. President, I would like to introduce Dr. Matthew Miller, known as Matt, and General Miller of whom I spoke. Gentlemen, this is President Strong.*

Matt and the General acknowledge the President without shaking his hand.

The President: *Welcome gentlemen. Thank you for coming to our assistance. You have been suggested by Director Clark, and I am sure you can solve the problem. It is actually my problem that affects the United States and possibly the whole world. Life must go on and I have to address the Security Council. He and George Benson, my lifetime assistant, will describe the situation. Thus far, we having no solution and some decisions must be made. So we wish you the best of luck.*

You have the assistance of the entire nation, But they don't know it yet.

The President leaves the office rather hesitantly, looking back as he leaves.

Director Clark: *Thanks to you Matt and the General for responding to my request. This is really a big deal and even war is not this urgent. Here is the story from the beginning up until we ran out of manageable options. The description is pretty long, so hold on to your helmets.*

Matt: *I think he is serious. (To the General but load enough so that Clark can hear it.)*

Director Clark: *You're right there. Believe me. This is all true. I was there. Air Force One was readied in a hurry and the pilots were rounded up; the President and the Vice President, along with a minimal service staff, were on board and the specially designed Boeing 747 airplane was headed to California in a hurry. Having the President and the Vice President on the same flight caused some concern with the Secret Service, who were overruled by the President. The planes headed to San Jose at the maximum speed of 600 miles per hour at 40,00 feet. The President's life-long friend and former Chief of Staff was dying and the President and his friend had made a pact to be at the other's bedside if death were imminent. The friend was dying of liver disease and wasn't expected to last the day. A few hours after the President arrived, the friend passed away, and Air Force One headed back to Washington. The President always returned home to the White House every night. He never slept away from his residence. Of course, there were exceptions for international trips.*

Director Clark took a pause for a drink of water, and then continued.

Director Clark: *When the President arrived back at the White House, it was late and he retired to a separable room in the presidential suite. He didn't want to wake the First Lady, who was nursing a bad case of the flu. The next morning, the President awakened early to read the President Daily Brief (PDB) and learned the First Lady was not there. The President, used to having everything just so, went into the panic mode and called the Secret Service. The President also called his trusted advisors to an urgent secret meeting in the blue room of the White House. The instructions were: (1) Find the First Lady, and (2) Keep the search a total secret from everyone. No one is to know in the U.S. and in the outside world. The logic was that the American people would be in a panic, the stock market would take am nose dive, and the news media would turn the situation into a frenzy. Several agencies would take care of the search and not tell anyone exactly why they were doing what they were doing. The known agencies are FBI, CIA, NSA, Police Departments, Military Intelligence, and special units from the Marines and the Army. The Chairman of the Joint Chiefs of Staff, a four star general, and I were consulted in total secrecy. In less than a week of search, there was no success. That was why and when I called you while in flight. Let me take a 5 minute break and get a cup of coffee. Then I will call in George Benson, the Presidents long time assistant, and he will continue with what has been done so far.*

The Director presses a button and a team brings in coffee and some fruit breakfast snacks. The scene continues in only a few seconds.

Director's note: *This is a very long dialog. It will probably have to be dubbed in, as in movies. This may be applicable in other instances in this script.*

George Benson: *Hello, my name is George Benson. The President has asked my to solve a problem of a secret nature. I have worked for and with him for more than twenty years.*

The General, Matt, and Director Clark introduce themselves. Benson does not look impressed.

George Benson: *The problem is that the President returned from a quick trip to California and as the hour was late, decided to sleep in an extra bedroom. The President always sleeps at home when in the States. The First Lady was ill and he decided not to disturb her. After PDB, the President was told that the First Lady was nowhere to be found. Neither the First Lady nor her Secret Service Agent could be found. The President had an emergence meeting and summoned the FBI, CIA, NSA, Military Intelligence, and local Police. The White House has been thoroughly searched. The military was put on alert. Evacuation routes and traveling routes were addressed. That included every form of transportation were checked. That necessarily included airports, train stationed, automobile routes, toll stations, border control, hotels, and other establishments. Even restaurants. The President thinks she was kidnapped but the FBI said absolutely not. We are at a dead end. He said that it persisted, he would have to tell the people, and that would be an disaster.*

Matt: *We can solve your problem. It's easy. You are looking where she could or should be. You should be looking where she shouldn't be. Then we will find her, and she will probably*

*be close by. Have you checked the wartime bunkers? The map
says there is one beneath the Treasury. Let's take a look at the
Treasury Building.*

END OF SCENE TEN
ACT II

Scene Eleven.

The characters are George Benson, Matt, and the General. Some Army Engineers are used as the scene progresses. The First Lady and the Secret Service are found alive and well.

On the way to the Treasury Building, the group notices there is a tunnel between the White House and the Treasury Building. Along the side of the tunnel, Matt noticed many closed and locked rooms labeled Cat Room #xx, for use by support people in the event of an attack. It was said they were stocked with water and k-rations. No keys to the rooms were were known to exist.

Matt looks at Benson straighr in the eye.

Matt: *You should get the Army Corps of Engineers in here and open the doors. Do it now!*

Benson surprised by such authoritative and rough talk did just that. The corp men were there is a second. (This is a play, not real life. Actually, it would probably take an hour.)

Matt: (To the engineers). *Open the first door.*

The room was empty but contained supplies and water.

Army Sargent: *Empty Sir, what should we do?*

Matt should look at the men like they are complete idiots.

Matt: *Look at the handles and see if there is a one that is a little clean.*

The Army men do that and find a clean handle.

Matt: *Open it!!*

The door is opened and there sits the First Lady and the Secret Service agent.

Matt is tall, slender, and tanned from golfing. He speaks with a calm and reassuring tone that makes a person respect him.

Matt: *We've been looking for you. A few people are getting worried. How did you get in here?*

Secret Service Agent: *I have a key from World War II in the 1940s. Several of us were stationed here. I know I don't look that old, but I am.*

Matt: *Next Ma'am, why are you here? I won't tell anyone. It's only between you and me. But don't worry, I'll fix things up for you.*

The First Lady: *I just have this awful flu and look at me. I look like a witch. I have been blubbering all over the place. I've been crying and my hair is a total mess.*

Matt says to the Secret Service agent.

Matt: *Why I the devil did you do it?*

Secret Service Agent: *Because she asked me to do it. That's my job. I am required to do whatever she requests.*

Matt goes out of the cot room and asks Benson to call the President.

Matt: *Tell him that the First Lady has been found and to come to cot room #37 with her raincoat and hat. Pronto!*

The President arrives in less than 10 minutes. Matt says to him:

Matt: *Be kind to her Mr. President. She needs you now.*

Some time later, Matt and the General meet with the President in his private office.

The President: *Thank you gentlemen. You've solved my crisis, and I will be eternally grateful. Please send me a bill for whatever amount you please.*

The General: *There is no need Mr. President. Our work is gratis.*

On the way home in the White House jet, both Matt and the General are very pleased.

Matt: *That certainly was a worthwhile trip.*

The General: *It was indeed.*

Matt: *I could use a round of golf.*

The General: *Sound good to me.*

To the Director fom the Author: *Life is Good. Don't you think.*

END OF SCENE ELEVEN
END OF ACT II

ACT III
The Escape

<u>**Scene One.**</u>

The characters are Matt. The General, Ashley, and Anna. Also, a man and lady at an adjacent table.

It is morning, and Ashley is in bed and Matt is standing at the edge of the bed. He is informally dressed for the day. She is covered with bed clothes.

Matt: Would you like a cup of coffee?

Ashley rolls over and looks at him.

Ashley: *Sure, I would love a cup of coffee. I thought you were going golfing this morning with the General.*

Matt: *He cancelled out at the last minute. I have no idea of what is going on. He called this morning at six o'cock AM and said he was too busy. He asked about an afternoon time. I said okay*

Ashley: *Both he and Anna have been acting strange lately. Maybe it's old age.*

To the Audience from the Director: *Matt and Ashley are married and long time friends. The had met in Dr. Marguarite Purgoine's creative writing course when they were students. Marguarite Purgoine is referred to as Anna for some unknown reason. She is married to Les Miller, known as the General, who served in the military as a General and was a decorated* *officer. Matt Miller is a well known mathematician and a professor at a prestigious university. Ashley is a former actress and teaches drama at a local community college. The General is wealthy through a political polling company and likes to help people and organizations. Both Matt and Ashley are tenured full professors with a liberal amount of freedom. Matt and the General enjoy their round of golf, but the general has very little say. Finally, after the ninth hole, at the resting area and restrooms, Matt asks what is going on. The General looks and says the following:*

The General: Something has come up and they want us at the White House as soon as we are free. Let's continue discussion this evening at the Green Room. That is, the four of us.

The dinner at the Green Room was extremely pleasant, and the subject of serious problems was not discussed. A pleasant man and woman, seated at a nearby table had the following to say:

Adjacent Woman: *I wonder what those people do to pass their time. The older couple does not even have a wrinkle on their faces, and the younger couple looks like movie stars. They are all slim and tanned.*

Adjacent Man: *They must be pretty wealthy, they didn't get a check and the younger man left a tip of fifty dollars. They also have an expensive Tesla parked in front.*

END OF SCENE ONE
ACT III

Scene Two.

The characters are Matt, Ashley, Ann Clark (The Director of Intelligence's wife).

Early the next morning, Matt and the General have their usual round of golf. Matt returns home and Ashley was waiting at the door. The scene is the inside of a door in a home.

Ashley: *I received a call from Ann, and she needs to talk with me this afternoon.*

Matt: *Must be important. What's it about.*

Ashley: *Don't know. She's taking the White House jet to the Newark Airport, and I have to pick her up from there. She said she will be available at the airport at 11:30 today.*

Matt: *I'll take off and be at the driving range. It is not my business, so send me a text message when she is gone.*

Ashley: *Why are you leaving? We know each other's business.*

Matt: *No, she wants to talk to you. Otherwise, she would have mentioned me. Something has come up. I'm glad we are on sabbatical. I bet someone has something for us to do.*

The. Stage segues from home to car with a slight movement of the backdrop. (This is a unique tactic.)

Ann arrived as planned and Ashley picked her up at the Newark International Airport in Matt's Porsche Taycan electric vehicle.

Ann: *I can't hear the engine.*

Ashley: *That's because it has an electric motor.*

Ann: *Oh, I didn't know. It's hard to keep up with cars.*

Ashley: *There's a lot going on these days. With global warning and the tense international situation, there is always something new. Conflict feeds invention, just like in World War II.*

They continued to Ashley and Matt's house, and when they got there, Ann digs into the business at hand.

The scene segues into a living room. (To the director: you are making stagecraft history.)

Ann: *I'm sorry to be abrupt. I'm here on very serious business. My message to you is directly from Mark as an order from the Director of Intelligence.*

Ashley: *It must be very serious.*

Ann: *Prince Michael is gone, so so is his son, The Prince of Bordeaux, named Philip George William Charles.*

Ashley: *Again?*

Ann: *Yes again. The whole British Empire is worked up like it's a major war. The U.S. Ambassador to Britain called* the President at the White House, and the White House intelligence chief called Mark. They have no idea of who took them and where they are. The intelligence people think it is Iran, China, or Russia. It does not seem to be related to anything in particular.

Ashley: *It is Iran. The easiest solution is usually the best one.*

Ann: *You may be right, and the intelligence people seem to agree with you. We want you to help us solve the problem.*

Ashley: *Why me? I don't know anything about international terrorism.*

Ann: *They want you to obtain knowledge of the the language and the culture of Iran. Learn the Farsi language, dress like a Muslim, go to Iran to find out if the kid is there, and then bring him back. They won't know you are an American because you will have a burka over your head. The whole operation is on the QT, but I think they want Matt and the General to play foreign scientific or business people - probably middle eastern - and get Michael out. They have another plan for that.*

Ashley: *They sure are big on plans. Don't you think they should contact someone to find out if Iran did, in fact, do the dirty work first?*

Ann: *It's the government, they do what they want to do. They make the plan, choose the people, and then blame them if the plan doesn't work. They do that in business, as a matter of fact. Make up an idea. Hire a consultant and the blame her or him if it doesn't work.*

Ashley: *I'll talk to Matt and the General.*

Ann: Let me know today. Now I'm out of here. The White House jet is waiting at Newark International Airport. It's ready to go. This is our government in action. Can you drive me to Newark?

Ashley: *Sure. We can take Matt's Taycan. It's the car in which I picked you up.*

END OF SCENE TWO
ACT III

Harry Katzan Jr.

Scene Three.

The characters are Ashley, Ann, and Harry Steevens.

The scene is in the driver and passenger seats of a sporty car. Ann is seated in the drivers seat and Ashley is in the passenger seat. This is a dynamic scene. The car and passenger remain still and the scenery moves. They are talking to themselves. To the audience they are just moving their lips. They pass through a small town, the entrance to the highway, and on the highway, and the highway with a policeman at the driver's window.

The dialogue to the audience starts when the car is on the highway.

Ann: *This is an amazing car Ashley. Do you drive it very often. I know you have that fashionable Chevy.*

Ashley: *The Chevy is fast enough for me. Matt and the General have their boys toys and it keeps them happy. I surprised that neither of them has ever received a speeding ticket. However, I really like this Taycan and the General's Tesla. They are both a bit expensive, but if a person can afford them, they are a good buy. WATCH IT! People like to accelerate and the police are near the entrance of the highway.*

The ladies move back in their seats to simulate accelerating in the car. The siren goes off. (It's Harry, the girl chaser. Just kidding.}

Ann: *I did it. Darn. I don't think I can talk my way out of a ticket, but I do have a government driver's license. I'm looking* *at him from the side mirror. He is looking at the car. He seems to really like it. I think we are okay. He is taking off his cap.*

Harry: *Good afternoon ladies. Nice car you have. I drove one towards the end of last year. I stopped a couple of guys, a young one and an older one, and they let me take a drive in their new car. It was amazing empty day on the turnpike, and I took it up to 120 and then backed off. That was fast enough for me. I sorry mam, I have to ask to see your driver's license.*

Ann pulled out her government issued driver's license, and Harry said:

Harry: *I had one of these once.*

Harry looked inside the car at Ashley. Then did a double take.

Harry: *Are you Matt's Ashley?*

Ashley: *Yes it is Harry. Do you still wear your Beretta on your right ankle?*

Harry: *Sure do Ashley. Never leave home without it. Have a good day ladies. And Mrs. Clark, please drive a little more slowly.*

Ann and Harry exchanged business cards.

Ann: *We have a job for you Harry.*

Ashley: *Harry studied math with Matt. He was in government service but thought that doing mathematical analysis all day long was definitely not what he wanted to do. Harry also* *saved the life of a member of our team in another operation with quick thinking. Apparently, Harry carried an ankle Beretta and happened to use it at the right time by shooting an assassin in the shoulder.*

Ann slipped Harry's business card into her Kate Spade wristlet that contained a government issued sidearm.

Ann: *All I can say is that you and your various teams are impressive. Would you like to go over your proposed part of the latest project? That is, if you want to take the assignment that I mentioned.*

Ashley: *I will take it and enjoy it. Matt doesn't know it yet, but I am sure he will support me.*

END OF SCENE THREE
ACT III

Scene Four.

The characters are Ashley, Matt, and the General. Director Clark and two intelligence women are mentioned.

Ashley was home and sent an urgent message to Matt and in fifteen minutes, he was standing in front of her. Ashley was beside herself with concern. The scene is their home.

Ashley: *Prince Michael and his son are gone and they want me to retrieve the son. They expect me to pose like a Muslin woman, and retrieve Michael's Prince Philip or whatever he is called. We know that he is a surrogate son, and the Monarchy is totally unaware of that situation.*

Matt: *If you don't want to do it, I'll get you out of it. Don't worry.*

Ashley: *I think you are also part of it.*

Matt. *Holly smoke! I'll ask the General to find out whether or not we are in fact involved. They always contact him first, and then he turns it over to me, whatever the situation.*

Matt was known to keep his cool, often in the most trying conditions. Today was no exception. Matt had another round of golf scheduled with the General, so he decided to wait and see what the General had to say about the kidnapping situation, as it was described by Ashley, even though the description was rather sketchy.

END OF SCENE FOUR
ACT III

Scene Five.

The characters are Matt and the General. Director Clark is mentioned but does not physically participate in the scene.

Matt is being coy about why their interactions have been strange lately. He senses a problem and wants it to show itself in. It's own way.

Matt: *Things have been different lately. I know from past experience that something has come up. You cancelled out this morning and you have never done that before and you have not been very talkative.*

The General: *Well, a few things have come up. I got an urgent call from Director Clark this morning. Actually it was in the middle of the night. There are two major problems, maybe three, dealing with U.S. security: Iran is planning an operation on our shores and we need a person with the technical insight to solve the problem. The second is that Prince Michael is gone, i.e., not there for some reason. This is the second time he has been missing and this time, it is not of his choosing. Katherine Penelope Redford, the retired Queen, has called directly and asked for our help. Actually, she definitely wanted our attention, i.e., you, me, and Ashley. I think primarily, it is you.*

The General hesitated for a few seconds.

The General: *And the third is China, and specifically, what they know about us and what we don't know about them. The President is concerned, Director Clark is concerned, and I am concerned. I really do not know where all of these problems* are coming from all at the same time. Prince Michael is associated with two of them and China the third. Here is what I think. If we can resolve the Michael situation, I don't know a better word at the moment, I think we can wipe out the first two problems.

Matt: *I think we should try to find out what is going on with Ashley. She has been approached by Ann, Clark's wife, and I think she is a loose wire, and she is taking advantage of the fact that her husband is very busy at the moment.*

The General: *There is this ridiculous notion that 'What Ann wants, Ann gets". Not around here. If we are involved, we are running the show. We can protect ourselves and the country. I hope that Ashley will be there when we arrive.*

Matt: *I totally agree with you. Well stated, Sir.*

END OF SCENE FIVE
ACT III

Scene Six.

The characters are Ashley and Ann.

Ashley and Ann are in the car headed to the airport. She receives an announcement of the message system in the Taycan.

Communication System: *Colonel Clark. This is an announcement from HQ. Turn around and return to the household of Professor Miller. The is a direct order.*

Ann turns the Taycan around and heads back to Ashley's house. She starts talking to Ashley.

Ann: *This is a good chance Ashley to fill you in on the plan. We know a lot about you Ashley. We know you had a royal marriage and were married to Prince Michael, whatever a royal marriage is. We recognize that a royal marriage is not the same as a legal marriage and you had a surrogate baby. I am skipping a lot.*

Ann sneezes. She is nervous.

Ann continues: *Michael subsequently attended Oxford at then Queen"s request and received a PhD in astrophysics. Prince Michael went to the U.S. to work and returned to the UK under suspicious conditions. He went back to Oxford and directed rather important research on viruses and vaccines. He was awarded a knighthood. He was abducted by a foreign country - we think - and that country is probably Iran, to work on atomic energy or an advance aircraft of some kind. For example, the Russians are supposed to have a hypersonic* *missile under development and the Chinese are supposed to have a hypersonic fighter plane, but you never know what is truth and what is propaganda. Michael may have a talent for putting projects together and that is why they are interested in him. We have evidence that Michael is in Iran, who did the abduction. So, we are proceeding in. That direction. Actually, the father and the infant were taken at the same time and we have no knowledge if where they are. The infant is for ransom, we think, but you. Never know. The mole can and will help us, so he will blow his cover and have to be returned with the infant and Michael.*

Ashley: *Where do I fit in, and also Matt and the General.*

Ann continues again: *Getting qualified people to do the job would be impossible. That is why you and the others were selected. You are all* **quick studies**. *Do you know what that means?*

Ashley: *Of course. We learn fast and are not stupid.*

Ann for the last time: *The three of you will be acquainted with cultural thing about Iran and also the Farsi Language. That will be 3 weeks. You will be brought in as a Russian, and we can get credentials and fly in as Iranian's do. The men have a problem and probably Matt will have to work that out. He will also have to work out how all of you get extracted. We have the knowledge and resources to work that out. For your information, the General has been given a tentative plan for the extraction. Well, you're home. Thanks for the opportunity to drive such a nice car. To be honest with you, this is not my kind of work. The Director is on travel status and I am just trying to help out. The President gets* nervous, the Director gets nervous, and that is why we would like to depend on Matt. The General also gets nervous but is an excellent organizer. All that is left are you and Matt to sort out the big problem, what ever that is. I don't think you are in trouble, but if I inadvertently cause you a problem, I'm sorry. You are a very nice person.

END OF SCENE SIX.

ACT III

Scene Seven.

The characters are the General, Matt, Ashley, and Ann.

All of the characters arrive at Matt and Ashley's home at about the same time and convene in the living room. Ashley and Ann get there slightly before and arrange the seating. Ann immediately took over the leader ship role and irritated Matt and Ashley beyond belief. The leadership business by Ann will have to end now, thought Matt. The General runs our show. Matt looked over at Ashley, and it was obvious that she felt the same way. People generally think that their way is the right way, except for the Army way that they say is superior, except for the General officers. There is also a a General's way. The General interrupted Ann in her first sentence and, from then on, it was the General's show.

The General: *We are all here for a common cause. Some important people are missing and we are obligated to find them. I have a big plan. I do not who made it. I repeat, I do not know whom made it. In addition to then missing people, there are military grade weapons that are superior to those of then U.S. there are exercises going on over then Sea of Taiwan's, and the Russians say they have fighter plane that is superior to then F-35. So we have plenty to do.*

Ann: *We can't solve all of the problems at one time. Which do we cover first?*

The General: *It is the missing person or persons. England is involved in it, and the former Queen has contacted me personally. We will have Buzz Bunday working that end. I haven't talked to him personally. Prince Michael, the Oxford* scientist, has been abducted. We don't know for sure, as of now, that he is in Iran, probably against his wishes. He has a child with the former Princess that has been under the care of a Duke and Duchess of one of the Royal Kingdoms, and he is also missing. Both events took place at the same time, and the authorities believe they are related. We will solve there other problems when we get to them.

Matt: *Iran is a big place.*

Ashley: *Michael is practically useless. His only asset is his extreme intellectual capability. He lead the team that created the British vaccine during the pandemic.*

Ann: *Why would anyone abduct a young boy?*

The General: *Ransome. The Iranians are short of cash, as a nation, since the U.S. has cut off their cash flow in international markets.*

Matt: *Let's make a plan. As far as Michael is concerned, I see a few obvious problems, such as locating him, getting the persons that will do the extraction, and transportation in and out. We'll have to coordinate with Director Clark on this matter. It's going to be a very big and complicated job. It will cost someone a very large amount of money.*

The General: *Okay, Matt and I will take care of Michael, and Ann and Ashley will take care of Michael's missing boy that has been named Philip George William Charles by the British Monarchy. I've talked to Director Clark and he has government generated information on the subject. At this* *point, the group will disband. We will work as team and the government has unique plans on how to we should proceed.*

Matt and the General arrange to meet with the Director of Intelligence in Langley in two days.

END OF SCENE SEVEN
ACT III

Scene Eight.

The characters are Director Mark Clark, Matt, and the General.

The trio are meeting in intelligence direction facilities. Matt and the General have flown in for a meeting with Mark Clark. The men are seated in a sophisticated government room.

Director Clark: *Thanks for an early start, Gentlemen. I run a tight ship. There is a lot of work to be done around here, and too few people.*

The General: *It doesn't matter, Mark. We are used to getting out on the golf course early, so we are used to it.*

Director Clark: *You already know the drill. I am going to focus on the available resources, since you are familiar with what's going on in the country. I may give some some suggestions because we - the agency - have been working on the situation.*

Matt: *We want to get Prince Michael out of Iran, and you might know that is where he is. You probably have a connection, and I guess it is that Iranian guy from Hilton Head, who couldn't get anything right.*

Director Clark: *It is, and it is a direct result of your intelligence work.*

The General: *Do you want us to leave a strong message when we exit from Iran?*

Director Clark: *If you mean destruction of some kind, then the answer is 'yes'. We can't show very much power by just getting out of the place. We have open DOD contracts with almost all contractors including the Lehman Corporation. You have the complete resources of the United States and the allies with whom we are affiliated. The ball is totally in your hands. My wife Ann will interact with you on matters associated with the Royal baby named Prince Philip and subsequent assistance and actions involving the State of Israel.*

Matt: *Do we have access to facilities such as the military drone network?*

Director Clark: *You do. Why do you ask?*

Matt: *An idea just popped into my mind. I just wondered if they - referring to Iran - electronically monitor drones like they monitor traditional enemy aircraft entering their airspace.*

Director Clark: *They do not. Apparently, they think that since drones are slow and can be easily identified visually, protection from them is not necessary. They might be correct, since drones are tactically harmless.*

The General: *I feel this is an operation with the highest priority to our nation and should be analyzed carefully.*

Clark waited for the General to say something more, but apparently the General was finished.

Director Clark: *It is of the highest priority and it has been planned more carefully than anything we have done in recent* *years. You are expected at the White House, and Kenneth Strong, the President, will make himself immediately available to you. A car will take you to the airfield, a White House jet to Dulles, and the a Marine One helicopter to the White House. I'm sorry I have a President Daily Brief (PDB) meeting, and we have a strict deadline, so I have to stick around here.*

Both Matt and the General look impressed.

END OF SCENE EIGHT
ACT III

Scene Nine.

The characters are the President of the United States, Matt, the General, and Kimberly Scott.

The scene is the President's private office.

The President: *Greetings gentlemen. We have an important subject to discuss. But first, how have your lives been?*

Both Matt and the General just smiled. No answer was expected.

The President: *I have an important job for you and your team. An important incident has occurred for which we need your assistance. Prince Michael of England has been abducted, and In have received a personal call on the subject from each of the following: the King of the United Kingdom, the former queen HRH Kathrine Penelope Radford, the Prime Minister of England, and the U.S. Secretary of State. You already know the problem that we must find him and return him to England in perfect health.*

The President hesitated, as if to say. 'These guys know this already. Why am I here?' I could be eating breakfast.

The President: *Our primary ally is the United Kingdom, and our good relations with them depend on it. I need immediate attention and every resource in the world, under our control, is available.*

Matt: *Do we have a description of what has been accomplished so far? A few items have been mentioned, but the totality of the preliminary work must be much more than that. For example, we've heard several times that the Prince and his young son are in Iran. Is this assessment for sure true?*

The President: *Mark Clark, Director of Intelligence, has our results. All I do is to motivate people and pay the bills.*

The General: *Deadlines?*

The President looked as if to say, 'Is this guy that dumb?' He hesitated. Matt looked off to the side, as if he wan't there. Emphasize this for realism.

The President: *ASAP. There is no need to mention again how important this is. You guys are on your own. You are professionals. Just do your job.*

Somewhat irritated, the President got up and left the private office through the secret exit. He did not say a word.

Matt: *Let's get out of here. Enough has been said.*

Matt and the General wound their way to Marine One and back to Langley. The General tried to call Clark but was told he was on travel status. He was informed there was a packet of information on the project named ESCAPE, available through an analyst name Kimberly Scott. Kimberly was abrupt with the General when she was asked for the packet by the General.

Director decision: *Matt explain to Kimberly that the General was a war hero, and also getting older. For the first time, Matt realized that the General might be getting a little older, and he would have to compensate by carrying more of the burden. This should be evidenced by his behavior.*

END OF SCENE NINE
ACT III

Scene Ten.

The characters are Matt and the General.

On the flight from Langley to New Jersey, Matt is the Captain and the General is the First Officer. In the modern world, this means that Matt was flying their small plane. The General was sitting in the co-pilot's seat was was fast asleep. Matt had the small plane on auto and was thinking through the task at hand. He had a small notebook and was taking down notes. The scene changes dynamically from the airplane to a small office in Ashley and Matt's home. The General's housekeeper doesn't have a clearance.

The General wakes up.

Matt: *I took a few notes on our flight and I wonder what you think of them. Do you want to hear what I wrote down?*

The General: *I sure do. You are good at developing creative ideas. You are really outstanding at it. I'm better at planning and organizing. It comes with age. I know it.*

Matt: *At this point, we have knowledge of the problem and the U.S. resources, since we have Kimberly Scott. Some of the U.S. drones are designed and built at the Lehman Company, located in Seattle - especially the big drones. My idea is to have Lehman design and develop a manned drone, just like the one used in combat without the people. Sounds crazy, but I think it will work. The manned drones would fly over Iran and deliver a couple of agents to the ground - namely, you and me, disguised as Iranians. Perhaps, we might have to fast rope to the ground, but in either case we would be there.*

We could land in the Sukhoi air field, the one we have used before. Iran ordered a fleet of fighter planes from Russia and built a special field for them. Then Iran experienced a budget problem, because the U.S. blocked their bank funds, and the order was cancelled. The field - the runways and buildings - are unused and totally accessible.

The General: *I remember the air field.*

Matt: *We will learn the whereabout of Prince Michael through Atalus, who is now a U.S. mole. He is the Iranian terrorizer leader named Adam Benfield that was uncovered and is now a spy for the U.S. Subsequently, a manned drone, probably the same one, will pick up Prince Michael, the young infant, Ashley, Benfield, and both of us and transport us to Israel, and then on to our respective countries. We take Benfield because his cover will probably be known. We need information on the English individuals that are to be abducted from Iran, if there are any, and we can get that from Buzz Bunday in England. The biggest problem is together a drone modified - or built - by the Lehman Company in Seattle. It makes the unmanned version and could revise it for manned occupants.*

The General: *Lehman is not exactly waiting for us to request a whole aircraft, and it takes time to design and build things.*

Matt: *First, you must have heard that Lehman has an extensive workshop that can make any part in anyone of its products. They have been able to to do so because they use subcontractors and, once in a while, they are delinquent. If a bomber plane, for example, is one day late, Lehman is fined a million dollars. It is true. Lehman has never had to pay it. The U.S. government is a tough customer, hence the extensive* *machine shop. So, they can do it; all we have to do is determine what we want done. And, of course, they will figure out how to do it.*

The General: *We have the contract information through Kimberly Scott. I think you have used her before.*

END OF SCENE TEN
ACT III

Scene Eleven.

The characters are Matt, the General, Ashley, and Kimberly Scott. Kimberly Scott is unseen.

The group is seated in the living room of Matt and Ashley's home. Matt is holding his satellite phone; he has just contacted Kimberly.

Matt: *Hello Kimberly. This is Matt. Are you free to talk. I'm here at home with Ashley and the General.*

Kimberly: *I was expecting a call from you. I have a packet for you, deposited by a high-level group under the command of Director Clark. You are going to be surprised. I'm send you all of the information, but I can summarize it for you over the phone. Things have changed. First and foremost, the Lehman company has changed dramatically. They are running under control of AI, and practically everything is now automated. I'm not sure that you will like it. It was a total surprise to us.*

Matt: *Let's have it. It's better now than later.*

Kimberly: *They brought in a system called Stategate that runs the place now. Actually, Stategate brought itself in and runs the entire company. The management of the company tells Stategate what it wants to do and wherever to go, and Stategate figures out what to do and where to go. I feed that information into Stategate, after you tell me. If I am not here, you have to feed the information into a computer that simulates me. The company is a very large assembly line. If you want something and Stategate has it, it tells you where you can obtain it. You can also tell it what to do. If it doesn't* *have it, it will tell you how long it will take to make it, and where and when to pick up the result. Make a request and I will give you the place you can pick up the item. Generally, you have to tell it where and what you want to do with the result. Don't worry. It has safeguards. I'll stay on the line. Just work out what you want and I'll give you a quick response.*

Matt addresses Ashley and the General.

Matt: *If we want a manned drone, quick give me an answer. We can change it. She didn't say, but we can assume the system takes care of changes. After all, we are humans.*

The General: *We need a large manned drone, piloted by a human and copilot. Conventional seating.*

Ashley: *Add one baby seat.*

Matt: *Seats for The General, Ashley, Me, Prince Michael, Benfield, another mole, helper - probably Harry Stevens, plus baby and pilots. That came to 7 plus 2 pilots plus baby seats. One extra seat. Delivery to where? Israel drone base. Linear take off. Do we need an escort?*

The General: *Probably a F-117A supersonic based in a aircraft carrier with a AMRAAM rocket. Average kill distance of 5 miles. Complete destruction of the enemy. Just in case.*

Kimberly: *I heard all of that and I ran it as a test case. You can have one unit and a backup in the drone base in 4 weeks from the go signal plus 2 days familiarization. One more thing. Delivery is by 2 Jumbo C-17s. Another thing. No changes after 2 weeks. Is that it?*

Matt: *Is that a go, everyone?*

Everyone nodded in the affirmative.

Kimberly: *I can't see you Matt. Is that a yes?*

Matt: *Yes, it is a yes.*

Kimberly: *Good job team. You are on your way. Godspeed.*

Everyone was totally surprised.

The General: *Dinner at the Green Room? Let me ask Stategate. Just kidding.*

END OF SCENE ELEVEN.
ACT III

Scene Twelve.

The characters in this scene are Kimberly (unseen), Matt, Ashley, and the General.

The team of Matt, Ashley, and the General are gathered in the living room of Matt and Ashley's house. Matt calls Kimberly.

Matt: *Good morning Kimberly, how are things in Washington?*

Kimberly: *Things are fine here, the weather is good and my work load is light today. You have only one item left on your plan. Would you like for me to give you a heads up?*

Matt: *Yes. Just read it out loud, and then we will be on our way to Iran training.*

Kimberly: *The two training courses on Iranian affairs are essentially the same, except for the male and female segments. The first two weeks are a condensed version of the Farsi language, and everyday customs. The third week involves personal interactions. The lectures are hand on and the language is totally immersive, as are religious and social sectors. Methods of dressing and socio-personal relations are described in great detail. The days are organized to be long, tedious, and complicated. Practice sessions are involved as are living conditions. Living in Iran is quite pleasurable provided that a person behaves by the rules and has something to offer the country through intellect and basic knowledge. Computer skills could be quite profitable since the general knowledge of technology is not widespread. The male and female segments are totally different. The male segment* *covers military, government procedures, and social behavior. The female segment focuses on female dress, child care, and subservience in a closed society. The American courses are given in Nebraska for men and in Virginia's for women use mock ups of Iranian structure and operation.*

Good luck to you guys, Matt, Ashley, and then General. You will be changed people.

The three crusaders walk slowly of the set.

END OF SCENE TWELVE
ACT III

Scene Thirteen.

The characters are Matt, the General, and a lone student passer-by.

Matt and the General are dressed as Iranians and walking down the Main Street of the university town. They walked about one block, when they are interrupted by a student.

Student: *Excuse me Sir, are you related to Dr. Miller in the math department?*

Matt: *Yes, I'm his cousin and live in California. Just here for a family affair.*

Student: *You sure look like him.*

The General: *That was fast thinking.*

Matt: *Thanks. It was pretty cool. I have to admit.*

The General: *Do we have an escort for Ashley when she goes to Iran?*

Matt: *In the plan, it mentioned that Harry Steven would be the escort. Apparently, the former Queen Katherine Penelope Radford has selected him. That was the first I heard about that. I heard that Adam Benfield would have a female mole to take care of of her in Iran and escort her with the kid - I mean baby - to the pickup at the Sukhoi airport. She was that extra seat that Kimberly recorded. It's possible that Harry is to escort Ashley to Tehran and then return. Then the female mole would take over. It seems that everything is okay. Harry* can then travel to the Drone base in preparation for the retraction.

The General: *This is the most complicated project we have been on. We still have the Iran internals to work on. I think that is our job.*

Matt: *It is also a bit risky. We are going to need the help of Adam Benfield.*

END OF SCENE THIRTEEN
ACT III

Scene Fourteen.

The characters are Matt and Ashley.

After three strenuous weeks, Ashley and Matt met at their home. Both were glad to see each other. They were in a risky operation and both were on edge.

Ashley: *Are you going to play golf?*

Matt: *No, I'm going to spend as much time as possible at home with you. We will have a short time - possibly three days - and I want them to be worthwhile. Are you having any operational problems with your end.*

Ashley: *No, not even one. We will take a direct flight to London in three days and Atalus with the help of an associate will get me to the son. Then, a fast Mercedes S500 will take us to an airport - they call it the Sukhoi Airfield where a U.S. drone will pick us up. The two teams will meet in our flight in the drone to the Israel drone base. We will then board a fast military plane to London and meet up with Katherine Penelope Redford and the rest of the people in the Monarchy. I will relay the result of our operation to Kimberly Scott, and she will arrange a flight back to the states. That is what I've heard anyway.*

Matt: *That's essentially the same with us, except the target is Prince Michael. I heard from Kimberly Scott that Buzz will take care of everything in the return to the states. That's good enough for me.*

Ashley: *He's quite a guy.*

Matt: *He should be. He's getting $4 million, if not more, for his efforts.*

Ashley: *What about us?*

Matt: *The General said we should get at least $4 million, but probably more if the President is pleased beyond reason and the retired Queen is also pleased. I think they will be.*

Ashley: *I will be too.*

END OF SCENE FOURTEEN
ACT III

Scene Fifteen.

The only character in this scene is Matt. He talks to Buzz Bunday, who is only a voice.

The satellite call between Matt and Buzz is to double check that they are all on the same page. Several people were involved with making the master plan.

Matt: *Greeting Buzz. This is Matt calling to double check the operational details of the project.*

Buzz: *Glad our called Matt. I was getting a little worried, This operation is a big deal around here. The Monarch is like a leaky sponge. The retired Queen is involved. We are going to use Russian passports for Ashley and your man Harry Steven's. Isn't that a misspelling?*

Matt: *It's legit, Buzz. He's dependable, and sharp as a tick. He was an intelligence analyst but prefers action.*

Buzz: *Before we start, we turned this guy Atalus. He prefers the name Adam Benfield. He is your key person in Iran. Okay. Harry escorts Ashley on the flight to Tehran. Benfield has a female mole escort Ashley to where ever she is to reside. Benfield says he has that covered. To him, that means he has taken care of it. The female mole will introduce us to the kid. Okay, Prince Philip. Harry flies back to then states. This a passport game. Harry uses Russian for Iran and American to get back into the States. Is this satisfactory, so far.*

Matt: *Perfect so far.*

Buzz: *Harry flies back o the Sates and flies with you and the General to the secret Israel drone base. We use the General's Gulfstream. We have secured the two F22 pilots somebody mentioned. When we have a completed mission, it will be used for Israel to London transit and London to the States transport. Where are the drones and why do you have two of them?*

Matt: *The two drones will arrive the same day as 'we the people.'*

Buzz: *Why do you need two of them?*

Matt: *One is a decoy.*

A long pause.

Buzz: *How long do we wait there for you to return.*

Matt: *Don't know exactly. Probably less that 5 days. Could be 2.*

Buzz: *Anything else?*

Matt: *That's all from this end. You don't have to ask. The General mentioned 3 but I am giving you 4, plus a possible bonus from the Queen. I'm using U.S. dollars.*

Buzz: *Is it that much? Are you sure?*

Matt: *I'm sure Buzz. Thanks for your help.*

Buzz: *It's a pleasure Matt. Signing off.*

END OF SCENE FIFTEEN
ACT III

Scene Sixteen.

The characters are Ashley, Harry, Matt, and the General.

The groups were scheduled to leave at the same time from Newark International. Ashley and Harry were taking Lufthansa to London, with a one hour layover and then on to Tehran. They were scheduled to pick up their Russian passports from Buzz in London City Airport and then on to Tehran. Matt and the General were flying directly to the secret Israel drone base in the General's Gulfstream, fitted with long distant travel features. The General had secured the two former F-22 pilots.

The four travelers take a limo to the airport. The stage is set to look like a limo.

Matt: *I can hardly believe that we are actually on our way.*

Ashley: *I can believe it. This Iranian woman's costume is already driving me crazy. People will look at me. This is worse than terrible.*

Harry: *What about me, escorting a Muslim woman?*

Matt: *You should have stayed in school and got your PhD.*

Harry: *You did and you are just 5 feet away from me.*

The General: *I wish Anna were here to tell me that everything will turn out just fine.*

Harry: *Do we have food on this flight? I'm hungry already. You guys will get American food in Iran. They copy American with hamburgers and beer. I'm going on to Israel and I don't know about the food there. I'm sure they don't copy.*

The General: *There is plenty of food. Just go back and get it. The government isn't paying for a stewardess. Matt! Did you bring a math book?*

Matt: *Of course. You know me.*

The passengers were tired and soon fell asleep.

END OF SCENE SIXTEEN.

ACT III

Scene Seventeen.

The characters are Matt, the General, and Adam Benfield, also known as Atalus.

Matt and the General have ridden in the manned drone to Sukhoi Aid Field and were met by Adam Benfield in his new Mercedes S550 car. The men were pleased to meet each other, even though they had met previously on Hilton Head Island in South Carolina. Matt and the General were totally surprised. Their friend Atalus, as he was known, was the biggest failure in Iran's history, and here he is driving a Mercedes car to pick up spies. The General and Benfield are on friendly terms. All three are in the car.

The General: *Adam, what is going on? Here you are, picking up a couple of illegal people in a new Mercedes car?*

Benfield: *We Iranians are rich. I guess you didn't know that. Do you remember the Shah of Iran, as he was called. Those people that worked for Iran were suitably rewarded. Things have changed, but the internal structure remains. The shah took the advice of an excellent American Scholar who is now the President of a university with his name.*

The General: *I think that I know who he is referring to. I got my Master of Science in Computer Science there. I later worked with him on a business venture - that is - the President, not the Shah.*

Matt: *Now we know. It's a small world.*

Benfield: *I'm going to take you to our most luxurious hotel and pick you up at 7:00 am. We start early in Iran. Tomorrow, I will take you to Prince Michael. He is working on the pandemic epidemic - pardon my French, as they say in America - and is helping us develop a vaccine. The virus is a very big problem here, since there are no contries that will help us.*

Matt: *Now that is a surprise. We were told by our American intelligence sources that he was working on an atomic project, or something like that.*

The General: *Now the abduction makes sense.*

Benfield: *You may order what you want from room service. They like American food here. Even hamburgers and beer.*

END OF SCENE SEVENTEEN.
ACT III

Scene Eighteen.

The characters are Matt, the General, Benfield, Prince Michael.

Benfield picks up Matt and the General and the scene evolves into a conference room. Benfield arrives at 7:00 am. It is only a few miles to the conference room.

Benfield: *Have you had breakfast?*

The General: *We haven't. We slept late. It had been a long day for us.*

Benfield: *Pity. Our food is the best in the world. We copy. It is only a few miles to the biology research building. Every project has a building.*

The three enter a conference room that is practically empty. Benfield introduces Matt and the General to a few biological scientists, and Matt and the General get to use their Farsi. No one seems to be interested in them.

Benfield: *The scientists are Swiss. They act like they are better than everyone. They might be.*

In fifteen minutes or so, Prince Michael enters with two body guards and starts to lecture in English. The audience seems to understand English.

Matt and the General look at each other. Matt makes eye contact with Prince Michael, who recognizes Matt and flicks his eye. Matt and the Prince know each other.

The Prince's lecturer on viral science is well-prepared and very technical; it is not clear that the audience understands what is going on.

Matt: *I was talking to a guy who was assembling an Artificial Intelligence development group for a company in Switzerland, and he was interviewing people for his team. A young fellow introduced himself and said he wild like to be on the team. The AI asked him what he had done in AI, and the person responded that he had no experience and wasn't even sure what AI was. His boss had asked who was interested in AI and he came over. Maybe the men in the room are just interested.*

The General: *Could be the case.*

END OF SCENE EIGHTEEN.

ACT III

Scene Nineteen.

The characters are Benfield, Matt, the General, and Robert Peterson. Peterson is from Iran and has studied in the U.S.

The next morning, Benfield repeated the trip to the biology building with Matt and the General. The room was empty except for the trio. They were approached by a tall Iranian officer. He addressed the General.

Peterson: *Excuse me, do I know you? Did we attend the university together?*

The General looked at the officer and said.

The General: *Yes, you do. We were in the same master's class together. You were from Iran and your name is ...*

The General thought for a few seconds.

The General: *You are Robert Peterson, and your associate was John Evans, and you were both from Iran.*

Peterson: *That is true. My Iran name is different. I am the country's technology officer, equivalent to an American Vice President. I would like to talk to you.*

Matt recognized that their cover has been blown. He looked blank, but his brain went into high gear. He thought: we are in big trouble, real big trouble. I wonder about this guy Benfield. I am going to have to figure out a way of getting out of those situation. Matt was as cool as a cucumber.

The three men were escorted by a guard to a separate room. The Iran officer initiated the conversation.

Peterson: *My American studies enabled me to attain my high position. I can have you put in prison or even executed.*

The General swallowed and cleared his throat. Matt looked into his eyes and saw fear. To the Director: the audience knows it is going to turn out okay and perhaps a little humor would be in order. Accordingly, the General's pants are wet and it was even visible. It's a play, not real life. (Just a humorous touch to a sad scene.)

Matt: *We are here to extract Prince Michael. He was taken without his wishes by an agency in Iran.*

Peterson: *I know. I had it done.*

Matt: *Why didn't you ask him to be a consultant to your country?*

Peterson: *That is not the way thongs are done in Iran. In have no control over that.*

Peterson hesitated several seconds.

Peterson continues: *I have A PhD in mathematics from a university in California. I know of you. You are a string theory scholar. You are Matt Miller.*

The General: *Why did you do this?*

Peterson: *Our country is dying from the COVID virus, as you call it, and no country will provide us with a vaccine. We can pay for it.*

The General was totally flustered. Matt was still as cool as a cucumber.

Matt: *Can we make a deal?*

Peterson: *All options are open.*

Matt: *Can you exchange the four of us - The General, your friend Atalus, Prince Michael, and me - for a working vaccine for all of your country.*

Peterson: *I can do anything. I have the power to release you as soon as you guarantee the vaccine.*

Peterson was cool as a cucumber. The General has an amazed look. Must be the mathematics.

Matt: *I can give you an answer in minutes. If you can direct me outdoors, where I can make a satellite call to the U.S.A.*

Matt called Kimberly Scott on his wrist satellite phone. Kimberly understood the plan in seconds.

Kimberly: *We have plenty of vaccine. Let me call President Strong.*

Kimberly responded in five minutes.

Kimberly: *He will guarantee the vaccine free of charge to Iran if England will guarantee a nominal amount. Iran has*

80 million people. 60 millions are adults. We will guarantee 40 million if England will guarantee 20 million. As a side comment, he will guarantee all 60 million, if necessary. He felt that England should give a little. After all, this guy Michael is from England. I have to call Sir Bunday and he can contact the Prime Minister. Just give me a few minutes. Just a minute. I have a response. England will guarantee 20 million doses. The following is important to complete the transaction. We expect to transfer the vaccine in refrigerated trucks loaded into C17s. We can load our 40 million doses into two refrigerated trucks in one C17 and England can load their 20 million doses into one C17. The three trucks in two C-17s will be delivered to Iran to land at Sukhoi Airfield in two weeks - probably 10 days. Iran has to guarantee they will do diligence and provide sufficient medical staff handle the does of vaccine. We will provide two doctors and one nurse to train them. Who is your contact in Iran?

Matt: *Dr. Robert Peterson. He is VP of technology for the entire country, and educated in the States. What about the kids?*

Kimberly: *The President said that we will guarantee child support as it becomes necessary. Oh, one more thing. If two U.S. doctors and one nurse are insufficient, we will supplement that aspect of the agreement. So far, kids in Iran have not been affected.*

Kimberly: *We have Peterson in our database. By the way, this Sir Charles Buhday, known as Buzz, is a wonder. I asked him how much he is getting for his work. He said $4 million and I raised it to $5 million.*

Matt: *You're a genius and I nice person.*

Kimberly: *I know. Just doing my job. I hope to meet you. Some day.*

Matt returned to the separate room.

Matt: *Listen please. I have very good news. The united State and England have agreed to provide 60 million does of vaccine to the country of Iran. It will be loaded into 3 refrigerated trucks that will be transferred to Iran in 2 C-17 heavy duty aircraft. Two doctors and one nurse will also accompany the vaccine to assist the Iranian medical staff. It should arrive in 10 days at Suzhoi Airfield. Dr, Robert Peterson will be the key perfusion in the transaction.*

Matt, the General, Dr. Peterson, and Benfield, known in Iran as Atalus, all shook hands. The operation of the American team had done its job.

END OF SCENE NINETEEN.
ACT III

Scene Twenty.

This is a unique end to a play.

The characters are Ashley, Master Philip, and her female Iran escort were picked up in their luxurious quarters and to be transferred to Sukhoi Airfield. The occurs on the first day of then holy season.

The scene is without voice and depicts 3 persons entering a Mercedes sedan headed to Sukhoi Airfield.

At approximately the same time, Prince Michael, Matt, the General, and Benfield were picked up in another Mercedes

The second scene is without voice and depicts 4 passengers headed to the same location.

The third scene depicts Harry Steevens loading the 7 passengers into a drone.

The fourth scene, again without words, depicts 7 passengers and Harry unloading the drone in the Israel drone base.

All of the passengers wave to the audience and all yell 'Thank You. We couldn't have done it without you."

END OF SCENE TWENTY.
ACT III
END OF THE PLAY

About This Play

The play is an adaption of the accompanying novel entitled The Final Escape. The book and the play are all fictional. Absolutely nothing really exists and it is totally for entertainment.

The play is fungible. That means that it composition may and can be modified under the usual circumstances with stage plays. The three associated publications are:

The Final Escape book
The Stage Play of The Final Escape
The Script of The Final Escape

The The Final Escape book is intended for the producer and the director. The Stage Play of The Final Escape is intended for the director. The The Script of The Final Escape is for the characters. The script and its format are intended to be reproduced.

Three blank lines accompany each scene for obvious reasons. This applied only to the script. The play is written with the characters in mind. Some sequences are a little long. But actors are smart people in addition to being good looking, and can easily handle them.

The subject matter contains no sex, no violence, and no bad language. It is realistic in the presentation. It is suitable for general audiences, college plays, and high school productions.

This particular volume contains actors scripts. Actor segments are in italics typeface.

About The Author

The author is a professor who has also worked for Boeing, Oak Ridge National Laboratory, and IBM. He has written computer science books, business books, and several novels.

He is an avid runner and has competed 94 marathons, including Boston 13 times and New York 14 times. He and his wife have lived in Switzerland where he was a consultant and a professor specializing in Artificial Intelligence.

He loves plays and sees every one he gets the chance. New York and London are his favorite venues. Mousetrap is his favorite play.

A Few Books by Harry Katzan Jr.

Advanced Lessons in Artificial Intelligence

Conspectus of Artificial Intelligence

Artificial Intelligence is a Service

Strategy and AI

The Money Gate

The Money Affair

END OF THE BOOK

**The Script of
The FINAL ESCAPE
In Three Acts**

A Novel

The Final Escape

A Matt and the General Book

Harry Katzan Jr.

For Margaret, as always

Introduction

This novel, as in the previous twelve stories in the series involving Matt and the General, with the assistance of their associates and friends, Matt and the General combine their efforts to solve three major problems that involve the safety of the United States. In this instance. *Escape* is set in the beautiful area of middle New Jersey, the United States in general, and in several foreign countries.

As in the previous novels, Matt Miller, who has a PhD degree from a prestigious university, uses mathematical thinking and solid logic, along with the organizational ability of General Les Miller, his grandfather, to solve three major problems, recognized by the President and the Intelligence Director of the United States.

In this set of episodes, the action includes a governmental kidnapping, the problems of the military situation with China, and the ongoing situation with the worldwide pandemic. Throughout, the activity uses the knowledge of General Mark Clark, the President, and three important women including Ashley, who is Matt's wife, Anna, who is the General's wife, and Ann, who is General Clark's wife.

The scene changes rapidly, but always in the scope of no violence, no sex, and no bad language. The book typifies the conventional "beach" read in that the subject matter can be read as three separate stories.

This is the thirteenth book in the Matt and the General series. The sequence has been interrupted while the author tended to academic pursuits. Nevertheless, expect Matt and the General to return to action with their combination of sophisticated planning and intellectual activity. Enjoy reading the book. You deserve it.

The Author,
June 1, 2022

Prologue

This book starts off where the previous book in the series leaves off.

In Part I, *The Monarchy*, Prince Michael is missing as is his son. The Monarchy is in a panic. The retired queen, now named Katherine Penelope Radford through the efforts of the Royal Lexicographer, called her friend the General. The U.S. ambassador to the United Kingdom, called the President and the U.S. Chief of Intelligence. The U.S. militry goes on standby alert, and the 6th fleet is moved to the Middle Atlantic. An aircraft carrier is prepared for action in the midde east. The location of the missing persons is not known, but the Intelligence directorate thinks it has the footprint of an Iranian operation. They check with a mole in Tehran, the capital of Iran, and their suspicions are confirmed. The mole say that he can locate the royalty but then his cover would be blown and requests, in that case, to have an immediate extraction from Iran. Mark Clark, former four star general and former chairman of the joint chiefs of staff, now director of national intelligence and the President agree to his request and the project is underway. An overall plan is made and the General and his team are called into action. Two threads are identified: one to locate and grab the daughter and the other to locate and extract Prince Michael and the mole. Clark and the President agree that is a risky plan and the right people will be required. The General and his team are selected and his team is called into action. Matt makes an operational plan that would be costly but probably successful.

In Part II, *The Double Spy*, America's secret hypersonic space vehicle (HSV) had been unit tested and is ready to go into production. It is a costly venture but will protect the United States for an extended period of time. The President, through secret channels, often has inside information when there is a leak in U.S. security. In this instance, the President thinks there is a leak, and then China announced a similar project. The President thinks that the Chinese announcement is a carefully planned bit of propaganda. The HSV is a costly endeavor, and the President needs to know for sure if the Chinese has an comparable project. The General and his team are called into action, and Matt comes up with an ingenious solution.

In Part III, *The Final Project*, the President is up for election and needs an unbiased view of exactly going on with the pandemic. If a person looks at the news, all one gets is a point of view to start with and attestations from related scientists for that point of view. President Strong needs Dr. Matt to tell him what to do.

The novel picks up from Part I.

Characters in the Book

The General – Les Miller. Former military General and Humanitarian. P-51 pilot and World War II hero. Has bachelors, masters, and doctorate degrees.

Matthew (Matt) Miller – Professor of Mathematics. Has PhD degree. Grandson of the General. Sophisticated problem solver and strategist.

Ashley Wilson Miller – College friend of Matt Miller. Former Duchess of Bordeaux. Married to Matt Miller. Has Master's degree and is a Receiver of the National Medal of Freedom.

Marguerite Purgoine - Retired creative writing Professor and an associate of the team. Has PhD degree. Known as Anna for some unknown reason. Wife of the General.

General Clark - Mark Clark. Former Four Staar General and Chairman of the Joint Chiefs of Staff. Appointed to be U.S. Director of Intelligence.

Ann Clark – Wife of General Clark and associate of the team. Formerly combat colonel in the U.S. Army.

Sir Charles (Buzz) Bunday – P-51 pilot and Army Air Force buddy of Les Miller. Member of the British Security Service. Knight of the United Kingdom.

Kenneth Strong – President of the United States.

Elizabeth Strong – Wife of Kenneth Strong and is First Lady of the United States.

George Benson – Associate to the President and Chief of Staff.

Kimberly Scott – The Intelligence specialist of the U.S. Has PhD degree and an extensive pubs record.

Harry Steevens – Expert mathematician and former college friend of Matt Miller. Policeman in New Jersey.

Catherine Penelope Radford – Retired Queen of the United Kingdom and personal friend of the General.

Prince Michael (Davis) - Son of the Queen, educated at Oxford, and renowned astrophysicist and developer of an important pandemic vaccine. Has PhD degree.

Harp Thomes – Academic friend of Matt and professor of mathematics at ETH Zürich Switzerland. Has PhD degree.

Kimberly Jobsen Thomas – Wife of Harp Thomas and international banking consultant. Has MBA degree.

Alexi Belov – Russian Mathematician and professor at a prestigious U.S. university. Has PhD degree.

Dimitri Aplov – Russian Virologist at U.S. think tank. Has PhD degree.

Wuan Singh – Chinese Mathematician and professor at ETH. Has PhD degree.

Adam Benfield – Iranian terrorist leader known as Atalus. Spy for the United States and England. Has PhD degree.

Robert Peterson – Iranian director of technology. Former student associate of the General. Has PhD degree.

And a few others

The Book Landscape

Part III
The Final Project

Part I
The Monarchy

Chapter 1
Getting Started

"Would you like a cup of coffee?" asked Matt, to Ashley who rolled over and looked at him standing at the edge of the bed.

"Sure, I would love a cup of coffee," said Ashley, Matt's wife. "I thought you were going golfing this morning with the General."

"He cancelled out at the last minute," replied Matt. "I have no idea about what is going on. He called this morning at 6:00 am, and said he was too busy. He asked about an afternoon time. I said okay."

"Both he and Anna have been acting strange lately," continued Ashley. "Maybe it's old age."

Ashley and Matt are married and long-time friends. They had met in Dr. Marguarite Purgoine"s creative writing course when they were students. Marguarite Purgoine was referred to as Anna for some unknown reason. Matt was Anna's favorite student, and the rumor was that she had saved all of his homework. She was married to Les Miller, known as the General, a former P-51 pilot during World War II, who had retired from the Army as a four-star general, hence the nickname, 'the General.' What else would a decorated officer be called? Matt Miller is a well-known mathematician at a prestigious university, and Ashley teaches drama at a local community college. Both are tenured full professors with a liberal amount of academic freedom. The General was wealthy through a political polling company he had formed. He liked to use his wealth to help people and organizations through his governmental connections.

The General is Matt's grandfather, and they share a love of playing golf. They play a round of golf at least twice a week. Matt was an intercollegiate golf champion and had played remarkably well at the Masters as an amateur. The two couples have luxurious homes near their universities, business affiliations, and the country club, where they usually engage in their favorite pastime. The General owns an expensive restaurant named the Green Room, where Ashley, Anna, Matt, and the General meet with associates for business and pleasure.

The General met Anna through Ashley and Matt. They hit it off in a short time and were married. They had similar interests and were in similar positions in life. The team had collectively solved several important investigations based in the U.S. Governmental arena.

Matt is extremely intelligent and employed his intellect to lead the team on several episodes that involve others, such as Sir Charles (Buzz) Bunday, the General's P-51 wing man, the Queen of England, Prince Michael, and several other prominent people, such as the U.S. intelligence director and the President. In particular, the General has a good working relationship with Mark Clark, former chairman of the military's joint chiefs of staff, and President Kenneth Strong of the United States. Clark's wife Ann is a retired combat colonel and provides assistance to the team and also other government people.

The General is regularly engaged in assignments that involve various aspects of life at diverse points in the States, Europe, and Asia.

Back to the situation at hand. Matt and the General

enjoyed their afternoon of golf, but the General had very little to say. Finally, after the ninth hole, Matt asked what was going on.

What is so special about the ninth hole? The course is 18 holes and the ninth is half way. That is where the bathrooms are. There is nothing special about that.

"That wife of mine is trying to make a writer out of me," said the General in a despondent manner. "She says I have writing talent."

"You do," replied Matt. "It's evident in how you think and choose your words. It's how you express yourself."

Matt just looked at the General, who recognized that a serious conversation had just started.

"There is more to our conversation than just that, General," said Matt briskly. "Something is bothering you."

The General just looked at Matt. "You're right," he said. "Something has come up. Something that is very important, and the President wants us at the White House.as soon as we are free. I told him that you and Ashley were exhausted and needed some time off from your extra-curricular work. I told him that you and Ashley were out of town and couldn't be reached. I said that was possible because you and she are on sabbatical. I said you might be hiking in Grand Canyon."

"Does he know that I now have a wrist satellite phone?" asked Matt

"I don't think so," answered the General. "You didn't get yours until after we last saw him."

"This wrist satellite phone is the world's best invention," said Matt. "I will have to thank General Clark for getting me one."

That ended the conversation. Neither Matt nor the

General knew what to say next and didn't feel like talking any more.

"Let's continue the discussion this evening at the Green Room," said the General. "That is, the four of us."

"Sounds good to me," said Matt. "I don't feel like talking about anything important at the moment."

The dinner at the the Green Room was exceptionally pleasant, and the subject of serious problems was not even mentioned. Anna didn't even say a word about the General's writing.

As they left the restaurant, a lady at an adjacent table said to her husband, "I wonder what those people do to pass their time. The older couple does not even have a wrinkle on their faces, and the younger couple looks like movie stars. They are all slim and tanned." The man replied, "They must be pretty wealthy, they didn't get a check and the younger man left a tip of fifty dollars. They also have an expensive Tesla parked in front."

END OF CHAPTER ONE

Chapter 2
Serious Problems Emerge

Early the next morning, Matt and the General had their usual round of golf. When Matt got home, Ashley was waiting at the door.

"I received a call from Ann, and she needs to talk with me this afternoon," said Ashley.

"Must be important," said Matt. "What's it about?"

"Don't know," replied Ashley. "She's taking the White House jet to the Newark International Airport, and I have to pick her up from there. She said she will be at the airport at 11:30 today."

"I'll take off and be at the driving range," said Matt. "It is not my business, so send me a text message when she is gone."

"Why are you leaving?" asked Ashley. "We know each other's business."

"No, she wants to talk to you," replied Matt. "Otherwise, she would have mentioned me. Something has come up. I'm glad we are on sabbatical. I'd bet someone has something for us to do."

At exactly 11:30, Ann arrived at the airport as planned. She had a serious look on her face that was unusual for her. It was a short trip from Newark to Matt and Ashley's home. Ann loved the ride in Matt's Porsche Taycan electric vehicle.

"I can't hear the engine," said Ann.

"That's because it has an electric motor," replied Ashley.

"Oh, I didn't know," said Ann. "It's hard to keep up with cars."

"There's a lot going on these days," replied Ashley. "With

global warming and the tense international situation, there is always something new. Conflict feeds invention, just like in World War II."

They continued to Ashley and Matt's house engaging in friendly conversation. When they got there, Ann dug right into the business at hand.

"I'm sorry to be abrupt," said Ann. "I'm here on very serious business. My message to you is directly from Mark as an order from the Director of Intelligence."

"It must be really serious," said Ashley.

"Prince Michael is gone, and so is the son, the Prince of Bordeaux, named Philip George William Charles." Continued Ann.

"Again?" said Ashley with a surprised look on her face.

"Again," answered Ann "The whole British Emprise is worked up just like in a major war. The U.S. Ambassador to Britain called the President at the White House and the White House intelligence chief called Mark. They have no idea who took them and where they are."

"Does this have anything to do with the pandemic?' asked Ashley. Michael worked on a vaccine in England that is widely administered to the world-wide population."

"The Intelligence people think that it is Iran, China, or Russia," said Ann. "But, it's not related to the pandemic."

"It is Iran," replied Ashley. "The easiest solution is always the best one."

"You may be right," said Ann. "We want you to help solve thhe problem. The government has a plan."

"Why me?" asked Ashley. "I don't know anything about international terrorism."

"They want you to obtain knowledge of the language and the culture of Iran. Learn the Farsi language, dress like a Muslim, and get to Iran to find out if the kid is there, and then bring him back. They won't know you are an American because you have a burka over your head. The whole operation is on the QT, but I think they want Matt and the general to play foreign scientific or business people – probably middle-eastern – and get Michael out. They have another plan for that."

"They sure are big on plans." Said Ashley. "Don't you think they should contact someone to find out if Iran did, in fact, do the dirty work first?"

"It's the government," answered Ann. "They do what they want to do. They make the plan, choose the people, and then blame them if the plan doesn't work. They do that in business. Make up an idea. Hire a consultant, and then blame her or him if it doesn't work."

"I'll talk to Matt and the General," said Ashley.

"Let me know today," said Ann. "Now, I'm out of here. The White House jet is waiting at Newark International Airport. It's ready to go. This is our government in action. Can you drive me to Newark?"

"Sure," replied Ashley. "We can take Matt's Taycan."

* * *

On the way to Newark International Airport, Ann was having trouble with her speed. She crossed over Route 130 and drove through Hightstown, New Jersey. She got a look from local cops who decided against stopping her for fear of a court case involving a wealthy person with a Porsche Taycan. But the fun ended quickly as Ann accelerated when pulling on to Route 95N at exit 8. They were stopped within a half-mile by a New Jersey State Patrol Officer, who was more than surprised. He recognized

Ashley and the Taycan and smiled when looking at Ann's government identification. He mentioned that he once had a similar government identification and was currently on temporary duty with the New Jersey State Patrol, since the pandemic had caused personnel problems with the patrol's workforce. The officer said his name was Harry Steevens, and Ashley recognized the name with the extra letter e immediately. When Ashley asked Harry why he had left government service, Harry replied that even though his personnel reviews were excellent, he was totally bored doing mathematical analysis all day long. Harry mentioned that he had attended and graduated from the university studying math with Matt. Harry also mentioned he had driven the Taycan a couple of years ago. Ann took his business card and mentioned they had a job for him. Ann gave him her business card that contained her name and government phone number. The card contained no other information other than 'The United States of America.'

Ashley looked up. It was assuring to have a take charge leader. As Ashley and Ann accelerated away from Harry, Ashley mentioned that Harry had saved the life of member of their team in another operation with quick thinking. Apparently, Harry carried an ankle Beretta and happened to use it at the right time, by shooting an assassin in the shoulder.

Ann slipped Harry's business card into her Kate Spade wristlet that contained a government issued sidearm.

"All I can say," said Ann, "is that you and your various teams are impressive. Would you like to go over your proposed part of the latest project? That is, if you want to take the assignment I mentioned."

"I will take it and enjoy it," said Ashley. "Matt doesn't know it yet, but I am sure that he will support me."

* * *

Back home, Ashley sent an urgent message to Matt and in fifteen minutes, he was standing in front of her. She was besides herself with concern.

"Prince Michael and his son are gone, and they want me to retrieve the son," said Ashley. "They expect me to pose like a Muslim woman, and retrieve Michael's Prince Philip or whatever he is called. We know that he is a surrogate son, and the Monarchy is totally unaware of that situation."

"If you don't want to do it," said Matt, "I'll get you out of it. Don't worry."

"I think you are also part of it," added Ashley.

"Holy smoke," said Matt. "I'll ask the General to find out whether or not we are in fact involved. They always contact him first, and then he turns it over to me – whatever the situation."

* * *

"Matt was known to keep his cool, often in the most trying of conditions. Today was no exception. Matt had another round of golf scheduled with General, so he decided to wait and see what the General had to say about the kidnapping situation, as it was described by Ashley, even though the description was rather sketchy.

Out on the course, Matt and the General were accompanied by two women, thought to be Intelligence agency personnel. This had happened previously. As the saying went, 'If you were friends with the head of the agency, you also had many special friends of your own that you didn't know you had.'

After the ninth hole, where the bathroom is, Matt asked the General how Anna was doing. The General replied that she had opened her studio on Nassau street and had several adult students that wanted to learn how to write from a creative point of view. Anna had said that she preferred students, as teaching adults presented different challenges.

"Actually, I was wondering how she liked putting up with an old GOAT like you, who was exceedingly dynamic, said Matt. "I was referring to GOAT as the Greatest Of All Time, who were exceedingly dynamic working men or women, who spent 30 years, 9 to 6, in a constant state of activity. So early in the morning, they are ready to go."

"Well, I suppose there is some truth to that," replied the General. "Right out of a good night's sleep, I am usually ready to go."

"I hope we can return to our two rounds of golf each week," said Matt. "I really like being with you."

"It's the same for me, Matt," added the General. "I have a lot to tell you."

"Well, you might as well get started," continued Matt. "Our two golfing companions aren't paying attention to us."

"It's part of the system," said the General. "It's likely they are part of Mark Clark's team. I'm sure that simple fact is the basis of the intelligence system."

'That's what I thought," said Matt to himself.

"Well you can start by telling me the reason for postponing our golf date," said Matt. "You've never done that before."

"I got a call from Mark," remarked the General. "There

is a problem – actually three problems dealing with U.S. security.

* * *

Matt and the General continued with their conversation.

"As I was saying," said the General, "I got a call from Mark. There ae two major problems, maybe three, dealing with U.S. security: Iran is planning an operation on our shores, and we need a person to provide the technical insight to solve the problem. And the second is that Prince Michael is gone and this time, it is not of his choosing. Catherine Penelope Radford called directly and asked for our help. Actually, she definitely wanted our attention, and she was referring to you."

"Ashley and I are both on a one-year sabbatical," said Matt. "I'll ask her about her feelings on the new projects."

Matt and the General finished the round of golf and had a drink at the 19th hole. He then called Ashley, who had just finished with Ann and had returned home.

"How is it going?" asked Matt.

"Not bad," answered Ashley. "An interesting problem has arisen that you might like. Can't discuss it over the phone. Why did you call?"

"It's probably the same situation that you have," said Matt. "See you in ten minutes."

END OF CHAPTER TWO

Chapter 3
Ashley

"We know a lot about you Ashley," said Ann in route to Newark Aairport. "We know you had a royal marriage and were married to Prince Michael, whatever a royal marriage is. We recognoze that a royal marriage is not the same as a legal marriage and you had a surrogate baby. Note that we a skipping over an lot of in between material."

Ann continued, "Michael subsequently attended Oxford, at the Queen's request, and received a PhD in astrophysics. We recognize he is quite a brainy guy. Prince Michael went to the US to work and returned to the United Kingdom under suspicious conditions. He went back to Oxford and directed rather important research on viruses and vaccines. He was awarded a Knighthood for his work. He was abducted by a foreign country – we think – and that country is probably Iran, to work on atomic energy or advanced aircraft of some kind. For example, the Russians are supposed to have a hypersonic missile under development and the Chinese are supposed to have a hypersonic fighter plane, but you never know what is truth and what is propaganda. Prince Michael may have a talent for putting projects together and that is why they are interested in him. Maybe Iran needs help in developing a COVID vaccine of their own. We have evidence from a mole hidden away in Iran who has evidence that Michael is in Iran and the U.S. top notch intelligence analysts are almost sure it is Iran, who did the abduction. So we are proceeding in that direction. Actually the infant and the Prince were taken at the same time and we have no knowledge of where they are. The mole could help us, but will probably blow his cover, and would require an extraction with the Prince and the infant."

"This sounds exciting and challenging," said Ashley, "and I whole heartedly accept the opportunity of working on an important project."

"What about Matt and the General," asked Ann.

"I know both of them," said Ashley. "They will accept the challenge, especially Matt, who excels in hard problems – as he calls them That's the way math people talk.

"Let me give you some insight into the geographic aspect of the operation," continued Ann. "We are assuming that they are in Iran, so we returning them – so to speak – from Iran and the closest country we can ask to help us is Israel. We would move them by some means, undecided at the time, to Israel. There ae good reasons that I will cover later. They will be moved first to Israel and then on to England or the United States. The plan is that you would work on the securing the infant, and Matt and the General would work on Prince Michael. Their participation is only suggested at this time. Here is why you were selected for this task. We know about your achievements and awards and are confident you can do the job. A qualified person to do the job would be exceedingly hard to find. You will be trained in subversive techniques, called methodology, relevant to Iran, as well as the Parsi language. You are regarded a quick study and the techniques we need can be obtained in in short time – like two to four weeks. Cultural behavior will be covered as well as the language. Because of Iran's dress conventions, no one will recognize you as an American operator. The rescue operation will be executed at the specific request of the retired queen of England, now known as Katherine Penelope Radford."

Ann continued, "You, Matt, and the General will be employed by the United States Department and the country of Israel. The reward for your services will be substantial – we call it an honorarium – and in all probability, you will be able to continue with your current employment after the operation has been completed. We know you and Matt are on sabbatical for this school year. This is a highly classified operation, and few persons will even know of it. You will get no fame from your involvement in this operation, but you will receive a substantial financial amount. We expect that you will not be in an danger during the execution of the extraction. Matt and the General's task will be highly technical, and they would be in some danger if the procedure is not successful. The project will begin immediately after you return to your home or the General's home where you probably will be headed after you drop me off at the airport."

END OF CHAPTER THREE

Chapter 4
Matt and the General

Mark Clark, director of national intelligence, summoned Matt and the General to headquarters in Langley, Virginia. The operation was classed at the highest level of national security, which required face-to-face communications. Matt and the General decided to fly to to Langley by personal jet. The General requested a flight plan from Clark, and it was granted in a matter of minutes.

The General's two engine jet with advanced features for fast flight and a self-regulating auto pilot was ready for the trip to Virginia when Matt and General arrived at the local airport, their plane was ready for their short trip to Langley.

Matt was an experienced with thousands of flight hours, and the General was a military trained combat pilot who flew P-51s, B-25s, B-29s, and even an advanced B-52. He infrequently flew the small business jet, and usually relinquished the pleasure to Matt. The General was a 4-star general officer that gained advancement through accomplishments in military flight in war time conditions. He had bachelors, masters, and doctorate degrees. The General was married to Dr. Marguerite Purgoine, usually known as Anna for some unknown reason. Anna had been Matt and Ashley' creative writing professor in their undergraduate days.

Matt had a bachelors and PhD degrees from a prestigious American university. Most of the brain work of the General's team usually resulted from his advanced analytical thinking. He had many published books and papers to his credit. The General's first wife had passed away, and he was now married to Marguerite. Matt is married to Ashley, who is a professor at a local community college. Her specialty is drama.

The General made millions doing political polling and is currently an ordinary individual sho likes to help people and government entities. The name 'the General' stems from the question consisting of 'what do you call a person with a high record of accomplishment.'

The General's wing man in the P-51 era was Charles (Buzz) Bunday, currently a retired intelligence officer in England and a knight of the United Kingdom. Buss and the General were close friends and associates in most of their nefarious adventures. One of the most noteworthy of which is the methodology, as Air Force Captains, was the invention of reverse mathematics for enhancing the safety of P-51's in combat. After the invention of reverse mathematics, the General and an enlisted driver were driving through war torn England inspecting air bases and aided an English female officer whose truck had slid off the road. The woman turned out to be the eventual Queen of England who is now retired and known as Katherine Penelope Radford. As royalty, she had no credentials, such as a passport, driver's license, and even money. The men helped the woman and gave her chocolate and nylon stockings, as was the U.S. custom. The general, subsequently met the retired queen and escorted her to a day of shopping and dining. They became close friends, especially after she retired from active royal duty.

The Queen is the mother of Prince Michael who had American academic involvement and strong English accomplishment, especially in the area of a vaccine for the ongoing pandemic and other technical accomplishments in the complicated domain of astrophysics. He had directed a team to produce the vaccine and was quite well known in that regard.

Until this latest happening, Prince Michael was an internationally recognized scientist. In this instance, Prince Michael and his surrogate offspring had been abducted and are located in a foreign country, believed to be Iran with the aid of an American mole in the country. It was rumored he was involved with an atomic project supported by a third-world adversary, probably North Korea, but most likely Iran.

An associate of the General and a close personal friend was Mark Clark, retired a four-star general and currently the head of intelligence of the United States. As such, Clark had information, staff, and funds to perform a wide range of international demands. The Direct of Intelligence was the right-hand man of the President. The current operation has the highest level of national security and subsequent services on the project was without question mandatory. Matt and the General had many international connections in Germany, Switzerland, and Russia, as well as England.

* * *

"So now it's time you told me about the second adventure you have inherited from your friend and associate Mark Clark.," said Matt.

"It is and will be a distinct pleasure," said the General, who was seated in the first officer's position. Matt was the Captain, in flying terminology, and it was the Captain who flew the small airplane. "Prince Michael, the one we know from current royalty," continued the General, "has been abducted from his position as head of research and development at Oxford University. Moreover, his surrogate son is missing from the home of the royally assigned parents. His royal name is Philip George William Charles and is known as Master Philip."

"Well, I'll be," said Matt. "Our friend certainly gets around. How did we get involved?"

"My friend Katherine Penelope Radford called me personally, as well as Anna, Mark Clark, and the President," answered the General. "Then, to top it off, the head of security at the United Kingston's foreign office called the President who contacted me personally. To top it all off, the State Department and the military office of security were requested to take charge of whatever it is."

"So that is how Mark Clark got involved," continued Matt, "and his key resource is a gentleman named Les Miller, otherwise known as the General."

"Exactly," replied the General. "The situation gets even more complicated. A sweet young lady in the State Department, who knows the President's wife, recommended Ashley, because with a burka, Ashley could be easily disguised as a Muslim. As we speak, Ann, at Mark's request, is visiting Ashley in New Jersey. As you know or probably expect, what Ann wants, Ann gets. As a result, Mark accepted Ashley's involvement in the project."

"Well, I'll be," said Matt.

"You said that already," said the General. "A third time is in order. Ashley and Ann are heading up Route 95 in your Taycan and got pulled over by a cop who knows Ashley and also the car."

"Harry Steevens," replied Matt. "Well I'll be."

"Ann takes his card and declares we have a job for him," added the General. "What Ann wants, Ann gets."

"I'll work it all out," said Matt. "So far, we have taken care of all previous problems assigned to us. You know what Ashley says, 'The easiest solution is the best solution,' and we have additional methods that we employ."

"I hope you are right," said the General. "I didn't mention the second project."

"Well, I'll be." Said Matt. "What is the second problem that needs our attention."

It's China," answered the General. "We need to know if the new aircraft they recently announced is for real. But, it might be propaganda. Our job is to find out which it is."

"They have been running exercises in the area between Taiwan and China, and the Taiwanese are pretty worked up," said Matt. "at least, that is what I read. We can take care of that easily. I hope that it is. I'm beginning to think that mathematics research is definitely more pleasureful."

"You are probably right, said then General. "We have to prepare for landing in Langley. When we return from Langley, you and Ashley can stay at our home for a few days. We have a few things to discuss. Precise coordination is necessary for our upcoming work. We have time for a little golf."

END OF CHAPTER FOUR

Chapter 5
The Problem and the Plan

Ann was requested at the last minute to return with Ashley to the General's home, which is where they were when Matt and the General returned from the airport. Their meeting with Mark Clark was short and to the point. Matt gave Ashley a big American hug that the General viewed with some apprehension. He had experiences practically everything is his long and successful life, but relationships still mystified him, even though he is a nice guy who is easy to get along with. Ann immediately took over the leadership role that startled and irritated Matt and Ashley beyond belief.

The leadership business by Ann will have to end now, thought Matt. The General runs our show. Matt looked over at Ashley, and it was obvious that she felt the same wasy. People generally think that their way is the right way, except for the Army weapon that they say is supersior to what the U.S. that has it's own way, except for general officers. There is also a General's way. The General interrupted Ann in her first sentence and from then on, it was the General's show.

"We are all here for a common cause," said the General. "Some important people are missing and we are obligated to find them. Secondly, one of our adversaries supposedly has a military grade weapon that they say is superior to what the U.S. has. They are conducting exercises over the Sea of China, the Sea of Taiwan, or somewhere and have the Taiwan nation into having a panic attack. So we have plenty to do. Also, the Russians say they have a fighter plane that is superior to the F-35."

"We can't solve all of the problems at one time," said Ann. "Which one do we cover first?"

"It is the missing person, or persons," answered the General. "England is involved in it and the former Queen has contacted me personally. We will have Buzz Bunday, working that end. I haven't talked to him personally. Prince Michael, the Oxford scientist, has been abducted. We don't know for sure, as of now, and that he is in Iran, probably against his wishes. He had a child with the former Princess that h as been under the care of a Duke and Duchess of one of the Royal Kingdom, and is also missing. Both events took place at the same time and the authorities believe they are related. We will solve the other progbblems when we get to them."

"Iran is a big pace," said Matt.

"Michael is practically useless," said Ashley. "His only asset is his extreme intellectual capability. He led the team that created the British vaccine during the worldwide pandemic."

"Why would anyone abduct a young boy?" asked Ann.

"Ransome," replied the General. "The Iranians are short of cash, as a nation, since the U.S. has cut off their cash flow in international markets."

"Let's make a plan," said Matt. "As far as Michael is concerned, I see a few obvious problems, such as locating him, getting the persons that will do the extraction, and transportation in and out. We'll have to coordinate with Director Clark on this matter. It's going to be a very big and complicated job."

"Okay," said the General. "Matt and I will take care of Michael, and Ashley and Ann can take care of the missing baby of Michael that has been named Philip George William

Charles, by the British Monarchy. I've talked to Director Clark, and he has government-generated information of the subject. At this time in the plan, the group will disband. Matt and I would work together, and Ashley and Ann would work together. As teams, we will be separated. The government has unique plans on how we should proceed."

Matt and the General arranged to discuss their ultimate plan that would depend on support from the Director of Intelligence. The General agreed to meet with Director Clark in Langley. The flight was planned for two days hence and lodging would be provided in the Intelligence facility.

"I think this is an impossible problem," said Matt. "Any information of value would be hidden in multiple layers of bureaucracy."

"We will work it out," answered the General. "The facilities of the U.S. Government are limitless."

The flight to Langley was pleasant. The sky was blue and there was little wind. The weather was perfect for for a round of golf – maybe two of them. But not today.

Director Clark liked to get started early, since the President Daily Brief (PDF) needed his approval. The Director's staff was excellent, and usually, the information was relevant to current events. The meeting of Matt, the General, and Clark was scheduled for 6:30 am. The lodging at the headquarters faclity was frequently used to facilitate an early start.

END OF CHAPTER FIVE

Chapter 6
Project Escape

"Thanks for an early start, Gentlemen," said the Director. "I run a very tight ship. There is a lot of work to be done around here, and too few people."

"It doesn't matter, Mark," said the General. "Were used to getting out on the golf course early, so we are used to it."

"You already know the drill," said the Director, "I am going to focus on the available resources, since you are familiar with what's going on iin the country. I may give some suggestions, because we – the agency – have been working on the situation."

"We want to get Prince Michael out of Iran, and you might know that is where he is," said Matt. "You probably have a connection and I guess it is that Iranian guy from Hilton Head, who couldn't get anything right."

"It is," said Clark, "and it is direct result of your intelligence work."

"Do you wnt us to leave a strong message when we exit from Iran?" asked the General.

"If you mean destruction of some kind," replied Clark, "then the answer is 'yes.' We can't show very much power by just getting in and out of the place. We have open DOD contracts with almost all contractors including the Lehman Corporation. You have the complete resources of the United States and the allies with whom we are affiliated. The ball is totally in your hands. My wife Ann will interact with you on matters associated with the royal baby named Prince Philip and subsequent assistance and action with State of Israel.

"Do we have access to facilities, such as the military drone network," asked Matt.

"You do," replied Clark. "Why do you ask?"

"An idea just popped into my mind," answered Matt. "I just wondered if they – referring to Iran – electronically monitor drones like they monitor traditional enemy aircraft entering their airspace."

"They do not," said Clark. "Apparently, they think that since drones are slow and can be easily identified visually, protection from them is not necessary. They might be correct, since drones are tactically harmless."

"I feel this is an operation with the highest priority to our nation and should be analyzed carefully," said the General.

"It is of the highest priority," answered Clark. "and it has been planned more carefully than anything we have done in recent years. You ae expected at the White House and Kenneth Strong, the President, will make himself immediately available to you. A car will take you to our airfield, a White House jet to Dulles, and then a Marine One helicopter to the White House. I'm sorry I have a President Daily Brief (PDB) meeting and we have a strict deadline, so I have to stick around here."

Matt and the General were escorted by way of White House executive transportation facilties to the private office of the President. Both Matt and the General were impressed.

* * *

"Greetings, gentlemen," said the President Kenneth Strong. "We have an important subject to discuss. But first, How have your lives been?"

Both Matt and the General just smiled. No answer was expected.

"I have an important job for you and your team," continued the President. "An important incident has occurred for which we need your assistance. Prince Michael of England has been abducted, and I have received a personal call on the subject from each of the following: the King of the United Kingdom, the former Queen HRH Katherine Penelope Radford, the prime minister of England, and the U.S. Secretary of State. You already know the problem that we must find him and return him to England in perfect health."

The President continued. "Our primary ally is the United Kingdom, and our good relations with them depend on it. I need immediate attention and every resource in the world, under our control, is available to you."

"Do we have a description of what has been accomplished so far?" said Matt. A few items have been mentioned, but the totality of the preliminary work must be much more than that. For example, we've heard several times that the Prince and his young son are in Iran. Is this assessment for sure true?"

"Mark Clark, Director of Intelligence, has oour results," answered the President. "All I do is to motivate people and pay the bills."

"Deadlines?" asked the General.

"ASAP," said the President. "There is no need to mention how important this is. You guys are on your own. You're professionals, and I have to monitor the the operation of the country, and do not have time to look after everything that happens."

The President got up from his chair and left the private office through its secret exit. He did not say a word.

Matt and the General looked at each other and made their way to Marine One and the return trip to Langley.

The General called Director Clark on his satellite phone and was informed that Clark was on his way to the Middle east, and there was a packet of information on the project named Escape, available from a senior analyst. Her name is Kimberly Scott. The notation emphasized that Kimberly could do anything necessary to the agency, and had access to a high secret information system that covered the U.S. and the outside world. Kimberly immediately liked Matt and effectively ignored the General.

On the flight from Langley to New Jersey, Matt mentioned that Kimberly ignored the General, who mentioned that he hadn't recognized it. Matt knew the General was hurt to the quick, and decided to do something about it.

Matt got Kimberly Scott alone on the satellite network for a few minutes and explained that the General was a war hero and a successful business executive. Moreover, Matt mentioned that the General was a close friend of the retired queen of England, now named Katherine Penelope Radford, by the Royal Lexicographer. When the General entered the conversation, the relationship had changed.

On the return flight to New Jersey, Matt put the plane on autopilot and looked through the Escape report supplied by the Intelligence office. Matt sat in the Captain's seat, and the General was asleep in the First Officer's position. Matt smiled to himself. He had a plan that he felt would surely work This was not unusual for Matt. He normally developed solutions in this manner.

After the return home, Matt and the General arranged

for a round of golf the next day. The General was tired but accepted. After a pleasureful round, the golfers stopped at the 19th hole for a light lunch. The General remarked, "Matt, you have something to want to tell me. Am I correct?"

"I do," said Matt. "I was hoping you would ask."

END OF CHAPTER SIX

Chapter 7
Matt Does It Again

The General sat back in his chair. He was sure that Matt had a plan and figured it would be exceptionally brilliant. Matt was a specialist in solving seemingly unsolvable problems. In this instance, the General had no idea about how to proceed on the problem referred to as **Problem #1**.

"I have an idea and please tell me what you think about it," said Matt. "I think it will work. I hope you will like it."

"I'm sure that it will," said the General.

"At this point," continued Matt, "we have knowledge of the problem and the U.S. resources, since we have Kimberly Scott. Some of the U.S. drones are designed and built at the Lehman Company, located up in Seattle – especially the big drones. My idea is to have Lehman design and develop a manned drone, just like the one used in combat without the people. Sounds crazy, but I think it will work. The manned drone would fly over Iran and deliver a couple of agents to the ground – namely, you and me, disguised as Iranians. Perhaps, we might have to fast rope to the ground, but in either case we would be there. We could land in the Sukhoi air field, the one we've used before. Iran ordered a fleet of Sukhoi fighter planes from Russia and built a special field for them. Then Iran experienced a budget problem, because the U.S. blocked their bank funds, and the order was cancelled. The field – the runways and buildings – are unused and totally accessible."

"I remember the air field," said the General.

Matt continued. "We will learn the whereabout of Prince Michael through Atalus, who is now a U.S. mole. He is the Iranian terrorist leader named Adam Benfield, that was uncovered and is now a spy for the U.S. Subsequently, a manned drone, probably the same one, will pick up Prince Michael, the young infant, Ashley, Benfield, and both of us and transport us to Israe, and then on to our respective countries. We take Benfield because his cover will probably be blown. We need information on the English individuals that are to be abducted from Iran and we can get that from Buzz Bunday in England. The biggest problem is to get a drone modified – or built – by the Lehman Company in Seattle. It makes the unmanned version and couild revise it for manned occupants."

"Lehman is not exactly waiating for us to request a whole aircraft," said the General, "and it takes time to design and build things."

"First, you must have heard that Lehman has an extensive workshop that can make any part in any one of their products," said Matt. "They have to be able to do so because they use subcontractors and once in a while, they are delinquent. If a bomber plane, for example, is one day late, Lehman is fined a million dollars. It is true. The U.S. government is a tough customer, hence their extensive machine shop. So they can do it; all we have to do is determine out what we want done. And, of course, how. I suppose they will figure out how."

"I have contact information on Kimberly Scott," replied the General. "She likes you and the two of you can makethe arrangements."

"Okay, give me her contact information," answered Matt, "and I will do it."

* * *

Matt and the General were transported by White House jet to Lehman field in Seattle. They brought no luggage as they expected a one-day meeting with Dr. Robert Bloomfield, the company president, a former NFL tight end, who earned his PhD from the University of Illinois. He had helped to turn Lehman into one of the most profitable and respected companies in the world.

Bloomfield met his guests at the White House jet as it landed at the Lehman airport and escorted them to his office. As Bloomfield, Matt, and the General passed between two tall buildings, Bloomfield pointed out the at the areas that were camouflaged during World War II for protection from enemy bombers.

Bloomfield's office was a duplicate of President Strong's office in the White House. Nothing was served in the meeting room and the guests were escorted by Bloomfield to their seats.

"Gentlemen, you have been recommended by the President and the Intelligence Chief concerning a high priority strategic mission," said Bloomfield. "I was told that the meeting would be technical, so I invited our Vice President of Engineering, Dr. Richard Robinson. We go by first names here. He will be along in a few minutes, since he has a strategic meeting with a representative of the U.S. Space Force. I am Bob and he is Dick, and I suspect you are Matt and Les. We know all about you, and will refer to you, Les, as the General."

The President of Lehman pressed a green button on his clean desk, and a guard escorted in Richard Robinson, the Chief Engineer.

"This is Dr. Richard Robinson, gentlemen, you may initiate the discussion," said Bloomfield.

"Our objective is to extract from Iran the Prince Michael of the United Kingdom and his son, and return them to their home country," said the General. "The operation is top secret before, during, and after the operation. Dr. Miller, known as Matt, will be in charge of the facilities, participants, and the operation of the events, and the interaction with Israel. It is important to emphasize that all activities, and every possible element of knowledge of it, are totally top secret. Violators will not be sanctioned by the U.S. Government. No operation within or for the sovereign domain of the U.S.A. has ever been performed, at least that we know of. Total secrecy is a strange phenomenon. You never know what you don't know. This applies to Lehman employees, as well."

"We totally understand," said Dick Robinson, the Chief Engineer. "I totally guarantee that you are not the first secret operation of which we have been involved."

"We were contacted by Kimberly Scott, who probably knows more about your operation than you would believe," said Bob Bloomfield. "Actually, we are quickly approaching the upper limit of the time we can spend on this project. General, you and Matt should now move into the technical phase of the project. Dick Robinson will represent the Lehman company and me in this regard."

"Okay, let's get going, continued the General. "Matt will go over the scope of the project and the technical requirements."

"We have to extract the Prince and his son from Iran,: said Matt. "Here is the scope are our requirements:

1. A drone to drop two operatives into Iran.
2. A drone to extract the Prince, son, female analyst, and 4 male analysts.

3. For time requirements, we should use the design of existing drones.
4. We will operate under a clear air route.
5. The range should be Iran to Israel and be escorted by an F-117.
6. The drone should be bullet proof.
7. The drone should use existing hardware.
8. The drone should use an autopilot with human intervention if necessary.
9. The drone should be indistinguishable from existing aircraft
10. The modified drone should be available in 3 weeks.

That's a brief overview of our requirements and you will have a description of the operational environment as we proceed. You may not receive additional information. The General and I will not be available doing other aspects of the project."

"We can do it," said Dick Robinson. "However, we will need information on the model being developed."

"Kimberly Scott will perform that function for us," said the General.

"Isn't that dangerous to have to have the knowledge necessary to do the project under the control of one person?" asked Robinson.

"Proceed carefully with your expectation in this regard," said Matt. "Our Kimberly Scott has a PhD from a prestigious university and has an outstanding pubs record. Her work is classified. Unfortunately, Kimberly is physically hampered through an aircraft accident and cannot walk. She works from a sophisticated information storage and access system. She has access to all government and human personal information in the U.S. She will be your contact."

"We will be totally unavailable for the next three weeks, and expect a working model at that time," said the General. "Is that possible and satisfactory?"

"It is possible and satisfactory," replied Dick Robinson, Chief Engineer, "and you can communicate thru Kimberly Scott."

Matt and the General were escorted across the highway to Lehman Field by an engineering aide. A White House jet was waiting. The next stop was New Jersey.

* * *

Matt and the General had time to talk on their way home. They were as relaxed as any two scientists could be under the circumstances.

"Now, I have something I have to tell you," said the General. "We are about to become international spies."

"That's quite a statement to a math professor," replied Matt. "This has to be a remarkable operation, so please talk slowly."

"You can pull out, remember that," said the General.

"You know I won't, so let's get going," replied Matt.

"We are both registered in an Iran school given by the intelligence directorate," answered the General. "We'll have two weeks on language and customs, and one week on social interaction given in our third week. After graduation, we will test our behavior on our hometown Nassau street. This is a crash course that has been well developed through the years."

"Should be interesting," said Matt. "When do we start?"

The General was totally amazed by Matt's seemingly calm behavior.

"Day after tomorrow," answered the General. "Ashley will start on the same day. We will be in Nebraska and she in Virginia. Kimberly has the details. The courses are similar."

END OF CHAPTER SEVEN

Chapter 8
The Plan Unfolds

The two training courses on Iranian affairs are essentially the same, except for the male and female segments. The first two weeks are a condensed version of the Farsi language, and everyday customs. The third week involved personal interactions. The lectures are hands-on and the language is totally immersible, as are religious and social sectors. Methods of dressing and socio-personal relations are described in great detail. The days are designed to be long, tedious, and complicated. Practice sessions were complicated as are living conditions. Living in Iran is quite pleasurable provided a person behaved by the rules and had something to offer the country through intellect and basic knowledge. Computer skills could be quite profitable since the general knowledge of technology was not widespread.

The male and female segments are totally different. The male segment covers military, government procedures, and social behavior. The female segment focuses on female dress, child care, and subservience in a closes society. The American courses given in Nebraska for men and in Virginia for women used mock ups of Iranian structure and operation.

There is an element of reality into the instruction after 3 intensive weeks, and Ashley, Matt, and the General returned to New Jersey as changed individuals. The men were even instructed in skin coloring so as to look more like Iranians. Matt and the General decided to test their Iranian presence and walk down Nassau Street in costume. The progression down Nassau Street went smoothly, but within a block Matt was stopped by a student who asked if he were related to Dr. Miller in the math department.

"I've heard that before," said Matt in broken English and was mentally prepared, saying the he was his cousin, who is the smart one in the family.

"That was fast thinking," said the General.

"I was prepared," answered Matt.

Masquerading as an Iranian was only a small part of the problem. Getting in and out of Iran was still an open item. Kimberly Scott had arranged through the former Queen of England Kathrine Penelope Radford to have Harry Steevens escort Ashley. Both would have fake Russian passports. Kimberly Scott was a whiz at getting things done. Matt had prepared for a seat in the drone for Harry's return. Harry didn't know that his honorarium for his services would be more than his salary for his entire life.

There was nothing on Matt and the General's entry to Iran, but Matt had prepared for that possibility. Kimberly did know that the development work on the drone was finished and could be viewed when appropriate. The General said they would go up to Seattle as soon as possible which the next day.

Matt and the General took a White House jet to Seattle leaving at 7:00 am the next day as anticipated. At the Nehman Company, they were met by Dr. Dick, as the Chief Engineer Dr. Richard Robinson, was called. He had a large golf cart, and they were transported to an area at the tail end of the facility. Getting in and out of the secret facility was as cumbersome as the Pentagon. The modified drone had six seats for adults and one child seat, as planned.

Matt and the General accepted the two drones and were told they would be transported by a U.S. C-17 cargo plane to the U.S. drone facility in Israel. Before they left the Nehman facility, Matt and the General were invited to a luncheon at the Lehman executive cafeteria. The Chief Engineer was more than curious about the project, but neither Matt or the General could say anything. During the luncheon, the Chief Engineer noted that the specially modified drones would be able to land and takeoff from a grassy plane analogous to a football field. He also mentioned that the drones could be autonomous or driven by a drone pilot.

On the flight from Seattle to New Jersey, Matt gave the General his plan for the entry and exit from Iran. His plan involved the assistance of Atalus, the Iranian turned American spy known as Adam Benfield in the U.S. Then General asked for details on the entry and the calling card from Adam, which referred to an incident, like an explosion at the Iranian facility, upon leaving. The General mentioned that he would ask Kimberly Scott to arrange for the interactions at the drone facility in Israel. Finally, the General expressed concern security and Matt said they could and would use an F-117A fighter plane stationed at an aircraft carrier. The F-117A was invisible to radar tracking. The General was pleased with Matt's work and was proud of him as his grandson. As the flight neared Hew Jersey, the General expressed concern over their entry into Iran. He was nervous and couldn't get over it. He was concerned over the specificity of getting into Iran and precisely how would they locate Prince Michael and his son.

* * *

After three strenuous weeks, Ashley and Matt met at their home. Both were glad to see each other. They were on a risky operation and both were on edge.

"Are you going to play golf?" asked Ashley.

"No, I'm going to spend as much time as possible at home with you," answered Matt. "We will have a short time – possibly three days – and I want them to be worthwhile. Are you having any operational problems with your end?"

"No, not even one," said Ashley. We take a direct flight to London in three days and Atalus with the help of an associate will get me to the son. Then a fast car Mercedes S500 wil take us to an airport – they call it the Sukhoi Airfield where a U.S. drone will pick us up. We will meet in our flight in the drone to the Israel drone base. We will then board a fast military plane to London and meet up with Katherine Penelope Radford and the rest of the people in the Monarchy. You and I may be on the same flight to London. I will relay the result of our operation to Kimberly Scott and she will get us back to the states."

"That's essentially the same with us, except the target is Prince Michael," said Matt. "I heard from Kimberly Scott that Buzz will take care of everything in the return to the states. That's good enough for me."

"He's quite a guy," said Ashley.

"He should be," said Matt. "He's getting $4 million for his efforts."

"What about us?" asked Ashley.

"The General said we would get at least $4 million, but probably more if the President is pleased beyond reason and the retired Queen is also pleased. I think they will be."

"I will be too," added Ashley.

END OF CHAPTER EIGHT

Chapter 9
Travel to Iran

"I have a couple of ideas," said Matt. "I need some time to put my thoughts together. How about a round of golf. I always think better when we are out on the course."

After the ninth hole, the General said, "Well Matt. Do you have anything?"

"I do," said Matt. "But I personally think that we can pull it more easily than one would imagine."

"Who or what should we use to do the job?" asked the General

The General was still extremely nervous about the total situation. Matt, on the other hand, was very calm and optimistic.

"We need an Iranian and one that direct us to the necessary site," said Matt. "We need someone to pull it off. You and I are to visible."

"How about Buzz?" replied the General. "Now that he is a Knight of the Royal Kingdom, he can and does get around. No one in Iran knows that he has a connection with us."

"Okay," said Matt. "He can establish a connection. With whom? The only guy we know is that guy Atalus from Hilton Head, as I mentioned. It's risky, since he seems to screw up everything he does. Remember? His American name is Adam Benfield."

"He is now a U.S. spy," said the General. "Mark Clark had him turned. He can locate Prince Michael and give us some assistance."

"I have it solidified now," answered Matt. "We can get in via the drone and Benfield – a that is his U.S. name – gets us to Michael to execute the abduction. Benfield can also arrange for the young son and Ashley. We can do it on an Iranian holiday. They pray a lot so security is marginal. We all meet at that unused airfield and the drone picks us up and takes us to Tel Aviv, is location of the U.S./Israel drone center."

"Do we publicize the assistance of Buzz Bunday," asked the General.

"We have that freedom," said Matt. "We do not really care who knows about the operation when we are finished. Perhaps, the President has some other thoughts on the subject. We probably should proceed with caution. Buzz, however, in not under any restrictions, provides he doesn't mention us. Matt Clark – I mean Kimberly Scott – can take care of that for us."

"What about the calling card?" asked the General.

"Just a simple explosion in the nuclear area would be satisfactory," answered Matt. "Just something to let them know that they have been hit but wouldn't result in an international incident. I do not like this calling card business at all. It's not such a mature idea, except in movies. There is no requirement that we do anything, and I think we should just let it ride. It's just another thing to do and we have enough things to do."

"Now that you mention it," said the General, "your logic sounds quite mature. I'll talk it over with Buzz, but I'm positively sure he will agree with you."

* * *

The General call Buzz on his satellite phone, who anwered on the first ring. "Sir Charles Bunday here, how can I help you? He had a smile on his face. He knew it was the General. He was a wartime buddy of the General. They flew P-51s together and Buzz was the General's wing man.

"It's me," said the General.

"I thought you would be calling," said Buzz. The project is all over London."

"So much for good American security," replied the General.

"Everyone important is involved," said Buzz. "The ex-queen Katherine Penelope Radford is also involved."

"I know," said the General. "She called me."

"Do you have a contact with that operator named Benfield? Asked Buzz.

"We do." Said the General. "We turned him."

"We turned him also," said Buzz. I am running him in the field, as they say. He can locate Prince Michael. He really gets around. This may be his last mission, since I think they are on to him. His cover has been blown. Iran only keeps him in the act because he knows a lot about American and British operations. Are you going to bring him in?"

"We are," said the General. "He is to valuable to them."

"How are you going to do it?" asked Buzz.

"Along with Prince Michael, his son whose name is Ashley, Matt, Harry Steevens, Benfield, and me in a military drone modified for the job," answered the General. "Actually, we have two drones, and one will be a decoy."

"It gives you a backup and protection,: said Buzz. "You American know how to do it right."

"Benfield should be asked to contact Matt, who will have the operational details," said the General. "Tell him to keep his mouth shut or we won't pay him and give him a new life in the States. Also, we are in a hurry."

"Okay, I'll have him contact Mat this PM," said Buzz. "When are you coming to England?"

"Once this is over, I'll probably visit Katherine Penelope Radford," said the General. "We should have the operation finished in a week, or so. We might get lucky."

"Boy, you Americans really get around," said Buzz. "I'll take you to a royal dinner when you're here. By the way, how much is this worth to Uncle Sam?"

"I thought you would never ask," answered the general. "I can get you $3 million, since this is a national security issue – so they think. I'll use your direct deposit number at the bank unless it has changed."

"It's the same," said Buzz, "and thanks. I'll be calling Matt about the project."

Buzz and the General were buddies during World War II and completed 35 sorties together.

* * *

Buzz Bunday called Matt on Matt's newly acquired satellite phone.

"Greeting Buzz," said Matt. "I just received my first satellite phone. Thanks for calling."

"Hi Matt," said Buzz. "This is not a pleasure call. But by the way, how are you and the academic world doing these days?"

"Things are going quite well," replied Matt. "I have published an advanced math book and several math publications. Ashley and I are on sabbatical this year. So we are free for the Prince Michael operation. We plan on getting into Iran and extracting Prince Michael and his son. We've completed our Iran training and now need assistance getting into Iran and the right place to extract the Prince. The only person we have in Iran is a turned U.S. spy named Atalus with a U.S. name of Adam Benfield. I'm thinking he can get us into Iran on a private flight or we can use some other method of transportation of our choice. We have some good options.

"I know him, Matt," added Buzz. "That joker is now a turned British spy, as well. If he can't do it, then nobody can. There is a possible problem. We think the Iran government is on his tail, and he might not be available to us. It would help if you could provide him with a safe exit from Iran.

"The U.S. Government thinks of everything Buzz." Said Matt. "We will provide him a safe exit. It's an important element of our plan. We are planning to use a drone for the exit, and there is a seat for him. One more thing. Could you arrange for a pickup at Sukhoi airfield over an Iran holy day? That's the day we wish to leave."

"Tell me about the airfield, Matt," answered Buzz. "Have you used it before?"

"We have, said Matt. "Iran built the airfield for a fleet of Russian built Sukhoi strike fighter planes that require special facilities. The financial plan fell through because worldwide banking facilities were not available to them, and there ws no need for the airfield. It was subsequently abandoned. We can use electronic location finding to locate it. We will leave with Michael, his son Prince Philip, Ashley, the General, me and Atalus, and perhaps an extea seat for another analyst. The drone is new and can be automatic or piloted. You can tell this to Atalus. He is guaranteed a safe U.S. location to live in, a new identity, and a lot of money after the mission has been completed. One more thing. Atalus has to also know where Michael and his are located in Iran."

"He does," said Buzz. "He told me he needs a retraction and money."

"To be specific, he is guaranteed a U.S. identity and $1.5 million," said Matt. "This is classed as an element of very high national security and the Presidential administration will pay. The reason of its importance to the U.S. – and probably the Brits – is their combined world position. You know, 'Hands across the sea' and all of that."

"When will this happen?" asked Buzz.

"Three days from now," answered Matt. "The contact point of the extraction has to be realizable to us."

"I'll let you know about the other details tis oses," said Buzz.

"Thanks, Buzz," said Matt. "I hope the General is paying you well."

"$3 Million," said Buzz."

"I'll get you #4 million," said Matt. "It's a tough mission and you need to be convinced to do it. Also, you are a Knight of the Royal Kingdom."

"See you buddy," said Buzz.

"Thanks, Buzz," replied Matt.

Matt's first use of his new satellite phone was a distinct success.

* * *

Matt called the General and mentioned the plan. The General was pleased and said he would correspond with Kimberly Scott over the female connection. He said a three day delay was necessary. Kimberly would have to arrange the Israel connection.

"We have to decide on point-to-point connections," said Matt. "We cannot have a U.S. drone just sitting there waiting for a pickup. We also need F-117A support for the drone. If Iran sends a chase plane, the F-117 would have to take it out. The F-117A is invisible to radar, and that is why we need its protection. It is advanced jet and is able to return to the carrier without a problem. Kimberly Scott would have to arrange this also. I don't thnk we have any knowledge on that subject."

"This is a lot of coordination for Kimberly," said the General.

"She will let us know if the connections cannot be made," said Matt. "I feel certain that it will be okay. She is an intelligent and sensitive person."

"You like her?" asked the General.

"I do," said Matt, "but only professionally. You know about me after all this time. You know I'm a straight shooter. I would say that Mathematician are as well."

"I was only kidding," said the General. "That's what some men say, trying to be humorous."

"I know," said Matt," but thanks again for the wrist satellite phone."

* * *

For security reasons that only he knew, Buzz Bunday, knight of the Royal Kingdom, arranged to use the General's Gulfstream G650 for the trip to London for the team of the General, Matt, Ashley, and Harry Steevens. He arranged for a secret air force base just north of London and the Captain and first officer were the the usual retired F-22 air force pilots. Harry Steevens was there to assist the others in making the connection to Iran. For her own security Ann Carter, wife of the Director of Intelligence did not accompany the team. Thus, the General, Matt, Ashley, and Harry were the only passengers on the Gulfstream.

The G650 left Langley at 10:00 pm and landed in London

the next morning. The airfield was practically deserted that gave an eerie atmosphere. Atalus had two planes lined up. The first was a commercial jet to Tehran, the capital of Iran. Kimberly had arranged for a valid Iran passport for Ashley. Ashley and the flight crew were to land at a public airport in Iran. Ashley was dressed as a standard Iranian woman. She was to be met by a female associate of Atalus and would be taken directly to the abducted Master Philip. It was intended that Ashley gain his confidence. He would be told that Ashley was his biological mother, and the fact that Ashley was a surrogate mother was not mentioned. Atalus' female assistant would handle the female operation until the eventual pickup by the U.S. drone.

Harry would arrange for Ashley's connection to Benfield's associate who would take a commercial airline to Iran. Kimberly would arrange to have an Iran passport for her. Harry would then proceed to Tel Aviv after Ashly were safety in route to Tehran. Harry, Matt, and the General would proceed to Tel Aviv in the Gulfstream. Harry would manage the preparation for the activity of the drone, and its trip to Iran of the General and Matt, The alternate commercial flight of the General and Matt to Iran had been scrubbed because their was concern that Matt and the General did not seen to look enough like an Iranian person. So, Matt and the General would take the Gulfstream to Israel and the drone to Sukhoi airfield. Information on the Iran Research Department would be supplied on the Mercedes S500 ride from Sukhoi to the secret technology center.

END OF CHAPTE NINE

Chapter 10
The Game Changes

Adam Benfield picked up Matt and the General at Sukhoi Airbase in his Mercedes S Class car. Matt and the General were totally surprised. Our friend Atalus, the biggest failure in Iran history drives an S class, and for routine tasks like picking up spies.

The General asked Benfield what was going on, and Benfield responded with, "We Iranians are rich. I guess you didn't know that. Do you remember the Shah of Iran, as he was called. Those people that worked for Iran were suitably rewarded. Things have changed, but the internal structure remains. The Shah took the advice of an excellent American scholar who is now the president of a university with his name."

"I think that I know who he was referring to," said the General. "I got my Master of Science in Computer Science there. I later worked with him on a business venture – that is, the president, not the Shah."

"Now we know," replied Matt. "It's a small world."

"I'm going to take you to our most luxurious hotel and pick you up at 7:00 am," said Benfield. "We start early in Iran. Tomorrow, I will take you to Prince Michael. He is working on the pandemic epidemic – pardon my French, as they say in America – and is helping us develop a vaccine. The virus is a very big problem here, since there are no countries that will help us."

"Now that's a surprise," said Matt to the General. "We were told by our American intelligence sources that he was working on an atomic project, or something like that."

"Now the abduction makes sense," added the General."

"You may order what you like from room service," said Benfield. They like American food here. Even hamburgers and beer."

* * *

The next morning, Benfield arrived at 7:00 am as planned. Matt and the General looed and acted tired.

"Have you had breakfast?" asked Benfield.

"We haven't," answered the General. "We slept late. It had been a long day for us."

"Pity," aid Benfield. "Our food is the best in the world. We copy."

It was only a few miles to the biology research building. "Every project has a building," said Benfield.

The three entered a conference room that was practically empty. Benfield introduced Matt and the General to a few biological scientists, and Matt and the General got to use their farsi. No one seemed interested in them. Benfield said the men were Swiss.

In fifteen minutes or so, Prince Michael entered with two body guards and started to lecture in English. The audience seemed to understand English.

Matt and the General just looked at each other. Matt made eye-contact with Prince Michael, who recognized Matt and flicked his eye. Matt and the Prince knew each other.

The Prince's lecture on viral science was well prepared and very technical; it was clear that the audience understood what was going on.

"I was talking to a guy who was assembling an Artificial Intelligence development group for a company in

Switzerland," said Matt, "and he was interviewing people for his team. A young fellow introduced himself and said he would like to be on the team. The AI guy asked him what he had done in AI, and the person responded that he had no experience and wasn't even sure what AI was. His boss had asked who was interested in AI and he came over. Maybe the men in the room are just interested."

"Could be," said the General.

The next morning, Benfield repeated the trip to the biology building. After about an hour, Matt and then General were approached by a tall Iranian officer.

"Excuse me, do I know you?" he said to the General. "Did we attend the university together?"

The General looked at the officer and said, "Yes you do. We were in the same master's class together. You were from Iran and your name is," the General thought for a few seconds and said, "you are Robert Peterson, and your associate student was John Evans, and you were both from Iran."

"That is true," said Robert Peterson. "My Iran name is different. I am the country's technology officer, equivalent to an American Vice President. I would like to talk to you."

Our cover has been blown, thought Matt. I wonder about this guy Benfield. We are in big trouble. Real big trouble. I'm going to have figure us out of this situation.

The four men were escorted by a guard to a separate room.

The Iranian technology officer initiated the conversation. "My American studies enabled me to attain my high position. I can have you put in prison or even executed."

The General swallowed and cleared his throat. Matt looked in to his eyes and he saw fear.

"We are here to extract Prince Michael," said Matt. "He was taken without his wishes by an agency in Iran."

"I know," said Peterson. "I had it done."

"Why didn't you ask him to be a consultant to your country? asked Matt.

"That is not the way things are done in Iran," said Peterson. "I have no control over that."

"I have a PhD in mathematics from a university in California," continued Peterson. "I know of you. You a string theory scholar. You are Matt Miller."

"Why did you do this?" asked the General.

"Our country is dying from the COVID virus, as you call it, and no country will provide us with a vaccine. We can pay for it."

The General was totally flustered. Matt was as cool as a cucumber.

"Can we make a deal?" asked Matt.

"All options are open," answered Peterson

"Can you exchange the four of us – the General, your friend Atalus, Prince Michael, and me for a working vaccine for all of your country," asked Matt.

"I can do anything," said Peterson. "I have the power to do the release as soon as you guarantee the vaccine."

"I can give you an answer in minutes," replied Matt. "If you will grant me an outdoors area where I can make a satellite call to the U.S."

* * *

Matt Matt called Kimberly Scott on his wrist satellite phone. Kimberly understood the plan in seconds.

"We have plenty of vaccine," said Kimberly. "Let me call President Strong."

Kimberly responded in five minutes.

"He will guarantee the vaccine free of charge to Iran if England will guarantee a nominal amount. Here are the figures. Iran has 80 million people. 60 million are adults. We will guarantee 40 million doses if England will guarantee 20 million. As a side comment, he will guarantee all 60 million if necessary. He felt England should give a little. After all, this guy Michael is from England. I have to call Sir Bunday and he can contact the Prime Minister. Just give me a few minutes. Just a minute. I have a response. England will guarantee 20 million doses. The following is important to complete the transaction. We expect to transfer the vaccine in refrigerated trucks loaded into C17s. We can load our 40 million doses into two refrigerated trucks in one C-17 and England can load their 20 million doses into one C-17. The three trucks in two C-17s will be delivered to Iran to land at Sukhoi Airfield in two weeks – probably 10 days. Iran has to guarantee they will do diligence and provide sufficient medical staff to handle the doses of vaccine. We will provide two doctors and one nurse to to train them. Who is your contact in Iran?"

"Dr. Robert Peterson," sadi Matt. "He is VP of technology for the entire country, and educated in the states."

"Okay," said Kimberly. "I have him in our database. By the way, this Sir Charles Bundday, known as Buzz, is a wonder. I asked him how much he is getting for his work. He said $3 million and I raised it to $4 million."

"You're a genius and a nice person," said Matt.

"I know," said Kimberly. "Just doing my job. Hope tp meet you some day."

* * *

Matt relayed the news to Robert Peterson, the General, and Benfield. Peterson was pleased beyond belief.

END OF CHAPTER TEN

Chapter 11
The Trip Home

At noon on the first day of the holy season, Ashley, Prince Philip, and her female Iran escort were picked up in their luxurious quarters and transported to Sukhoi Aarfield in a Mercedes amour plated S500. At the same approximate time, Prince Michael, Matt, the Gneral, and Adam Benfield were picked up in an identical vehicle.

At about the same time two American drones left Tel Aviv headed to the same airfield in Iran. One of the drones was a decoy. Again at the same time, a U.S. F-117A fighter jet took off from an aircraft carrier in the Persian Gulf and headed at an approximate mach 2 speed towards the same airfield.

An Iranian radar had picked up the drones and scrambled a Russian built fighter jet. It was picked up by the F-117A's radar and an advanced AIM-12 AMRAAM rocket destroyed the Iranian jet completely. The F-117A was invisible to the Iranian radar unit. The F-117A headed back to the carrier. Another days work eliminating an enemy the pilot never saw. So far, everything was proceeding as planned.

The specially built drone landed at the appointed spot at the agreed upon time in the Sukhoi Airfield. The door opened and Harry Steevens greeted the passengers. The drone flight to Israel was peaceful and no one seemed to even notice that Adam Benfield the U.S. turned mole was in the same aircraft. His cover had been lost and he would henceforth be a target of Iranian security police.

The General's Gulfstream G650 flew Ashley, Prince Michael, Prince Philip, Matt, the General, and Adam Benfield to London. The mission had been completed and the retired queesn, Katherine Penelope Radford, U.S. President Strong, and the U.S. Ambassador were pleased beyond expectation.

Sir Charles (Buzz) Bunday arranged for a typical British celebration dinner at the palace fot the 3 dignitaries and he 4 warriors, plus Prince Michael and his son. The retired queen and the General had their traditional get together at Harrods, the Ritz, and Simpson's on the Strand.

In the U.S. and worldwide, the omicron variant of the COVID-19 pandemic loomed its terrible head. Matt and the General knew they would be working with Prince Michael and the virus.

END OF CHAPTER ELEVEN AND PART I

Part II
The Double Spy

Chapter 12
The Chinese Problem

"Congratulations on your success with the Iranian problem," said President Kenneth Strong to Ashley, Matt, and the General. "I think you did an admirable job on the first of our three problems, and I think you should take a week off in Maui, or somewhere like that. The U.S. will pay for your vacation. Then you can get started on the Taiwan situation. On the surface, it seems like a straight forward problem, in that all we need is information on just what China is doing in the ever-changing world of ours, especially space technology.

"We're on top of it, Sir." said Matt. "All we need to do is get someone in the Chinese hierarchy and thereby get the information we need."

"Easier said than done," said the President."

"The first thing we need to do is finding out exactly what our Space Force is doing," replied Matt. I'll have Kimberly Scott get on it right away."

"Touch base with Kimberly when you're back," said the President. "Then get started on the project."

"Strong has changed to be as tough as nails," said the General on the White House jet to New Jersey.

"Not exactly," said Ashley. "He didn't tell us what he wanted. Usually the politicians tell you the information they want beforehand, and it is your job to get it and tell how you got it."

"Where did you get that opinion?" asked Matt.

"Ann," replied Ashley. "She knows and tell how the government works."

"Well," said Matt. "I think our work has already started."

* * *

Ashley, Matt, the General, and Anna did take a short vacation. They took the Gulfstream, owned by the General, to Maui for golf and shopping. The General asked Ann to accompany them, and she denied. "It wouldn't be proper," she said.

"I'll see about that," replied the general.

"The next morning, the Director of Intelligence, Mark Clark and his wife Ann, accompanied the other four on their trip to Maui.

While in Maui, the Director contacted Kimberly for as assessment of what the U.S. was doing in space that we are keeping top secret.

"It's the space plane, the V-35," said Kimberly. "The project is not secret but what it can do is very top secret. I would say the Chinese have heard of our combined space plane tht is supposed to consist of space vehicle, military done, high speed fighter, space supply ship, and booster – all in one. The Chinese are having fits and that is why they are overflying Taiwan air space and getting everyone all worked up."

"We should get to someone in the Chinese military hierarchy that knows what they are doing – I mean overall country, not a single person," said Matt. "I'll work on it. It should be easy to find someone with a Chinese connection in the academic world."

As it turned out, the week of vacation in Maui was a total waste of time, except for the golf. Other than Matt and the General, no one seemed to be interested in playing or doing anything. All the others did was eat, sleep, and work on their suntan. As they said, that is what vacations are for.

The COVID-19 variant named omicron was in the news, and everyone felt they were retty safe with two shots of vaccine and the booster would keep them secure as possible.

The calm of the vacation was changed when the General received a satellite call from Ssir Buzz Bunday. "Les, the people here are in a total panic over the omicron variant to COVID-19. It has terrorized London, and the city is in a lockdown, meaning persons are not allowed on the streets unless they are on purposeful business. Prince Michael is again the center of attention. He maintains that Iran has discovered the virus in South Africa, and they are working hard at making a nuisance of themselves hoping to change the U.S. restriction on Iranian financial transactions. They feel that it is of no use to sell the oil to the world when they can't spend the money. He is a professional nuisance."

Ashley looked up as if to say, 'I told you so.'

Only Matt had a response to Buzz's conjecture. "That explains a few things in our work order," he said. "I suppose that omicron situation will be next on our list of major problems."

* * *

"I think I'll call Harp Thomas," Matt said to the General.

"I don't remember Harp Thomas," said the General. "I have forgotten the name or never knew it."

"You probably never were exposed to it," answered Matt. "I think you were working on other things. Harper Thomas, known as Harp, was a buddy of mine in the PhD program in graduate school and is now a professor of math at ETH in Zürich. His wife is Kimberly Jobsen Thomas, consultant to a Swiss bank. She has an MBA and married Harp Thomas. I think you know her father. His name is Jobsen and is the millionaire floating around our area of New Jersey. Harp worked with us on a few projects and then went off to teach math at ETH, the Swiss university. As I said, he married Kimberly Jobsen, a daughter of a friend of yours. Back to the problem at hand. The ETH university has a lot of faculty coming and going. It is possible there is a person there from China that we can use. The Chinese love math and send faculty around the world to make sure they are totally up to date on latest developments. For example, they are extremely interested in my work on string theory."

"You might as well call your friend Harp," said the General. "It's a way to start the project, and I can't think of a better way."

* * *

"Harp, this is Matt. How are you and Kimberly doing these day?"

"I would say we are enjoying the family life of ours," said Harp. "I've wondered about you."

"We're on a special job for the U.S. government and could use your assistance," answered Matt. "The work is top secret and does not involve any danger and physical contact at all."

"I'm on," said Harp. "I've always enjoyed the little bit of excitement working with you."

"I need to handle this face-to-face so I propose that Ashley, the General, and I come to Zürich. The General and his wife will probably go to his residence in Klosters, and Ashley will probably join us during our sessions."

"Come anytime Matt," replied Harp. "You know about university free time, so we will probably have plenty of time together."

"How about tomorrow?" asked Matt. "We could be there by early evening."

"Okay," said Harp. "We live in the same apartment across the street from the Storchen hotel."

"Thanks, Harp," said Matt. "We'll be there tomorrow."

"I'll make a reservation for you at the Storchen," said Harp.

"Thanks again," said Matt, as he hung up.

* * *

"I set up a meeting with Harp in Zürich for toomorrow," said Matt.

"You don't waste any time," replied the General.

'Is it all right if you, Ashley, Anna, and I take the Gulfstream?", asked Matt. "I thought that perhaps Anna and you would like to spend some time in Klosters."

"When do we fly?" asked the General a little surprised.

"Tomorrow, so we get there in the evening," answered Matt.

Okay, I'll have the flight set up today so we can leave early in the morning. We can leave from Newark International Airport in the morning. We should leave early because their time is ahead of us – I think 6 hours. What about leaving the U.S. at 6 am and leaving here by limo at 5 am."

"You don't waste any time," said Matt. "We'll be here a 5 am."

* * *

Matt and Ashley dressed in business attire with one change of clothes. As usual, the General said that if they needed anything they could just buy it. They never did. The flight to Zürich was uneventful, as usual, and Kloten Airport was spick and spot, as they say it. The General ordered a limo, for the first time, the group was at the Storchen in no time. Switzerland was a very nice place.

Ashley, Anna, Matt, and the General checked in to the Storchen that was very accomodating and the rooms were immaculate. They had been redecorated and the group was the first guests to enjoy them.

The Thomas' apartment was just across the street. The size of the rooms were small, but exquisitely decorated. Kimberly Thomas answered the door with her usual smile, and a load of good cheer. Harp was right behind here. He acknowledged Ashley, Anna, and the General, but gave a warm welcome to Matt. They went through a tough PhD program together and would be close friends forever.

"Welcome to Zürich," said Harp. "You guys really look good. It's really nice to see an American. What can we do for you?"

"We – that is, our client the U.S. government – needs some information on China, and the President cannot wait for it to come through the Intelligence system," said Matt. "Do you happen to have a Chinese professor on your teaching staff? I know that ETH has an open door for foreign researchers in mathematics.

"We have two Chinese visiting faculty," said Harp. "One is my climbing buddy. He used to work on aerospace and defense, and now works on string theory and black holes. He's a bit miffed at China because they want him to be a spy for China against the U.S., and other countries, like the UK. He also likes money.

"I have an idea, Harp," said Matt. "Why couldn't run him as a double agent. He could obtain information for us and we could pass on misinformation to China. By the way, what is his name?"

"It is Wuan Singh," said Harp. "But I don't know in china where he is from. He's a good mountain climber."

"Hold on," said Matt. "I've find out what we need."

Matt got out his satellite phone and waited for a connection with Kimberly Scott in Intelligence.

"We have a system for finding out about people and places, "added Matt to the rest of the room."

"Hello Matt," said Kimberly. "How are you and where are you? I have to check out the connection."

"I'm in Zürich Switzerland," said Matt.

"Okay, what can I do for you?"

"Can you make a search on Wuan Singh, Chinese citizen, mathematician, mountain climber, at ETH in Switzerland, and friend of Harper Thomas, American," said Matt, "I'll hold on."

Matt's wrist satellite phone was in the speaker mode.

Kimberly Thomas looked at Ashley and said, "Is he always this sharp?"

"Seems to be," answered Ashley. "He's good at analytics."

Kimberly Scott came back online. "He is totally clean. He has a PhD from M.I.T. There is none more thing, Matt," continued Kimberly. "We have a line into the Chinese information system. They are performing the same person check for same reason – I expect. Are you going to create a double agent?"

"Could be," said Matt. "Probably."

"Do we have an M.I.T. *Nonper*," asked Matt.

"We do," said Kimberly. "We haven't used it yet."

"Thanks Kimberly," said Matt. "You're the best."

"I know," said Kimberly.

"What's a *Nonper*," asked Ashley.

"It's an identity for a person that doesn't exist." replied Matt.

END OF CHAPTER TWELVE

Chapter 13
The Chinese Solution

"Let me go over what we need to accomplish on the Chinese mission," said Matt. "We are all security classified, so you will understand that what we say or do is top secret to the United States."

Matt continues. "Here is the plan so far. The government needs to know what the country of China is doing in a particular area. We need a person to whom our country will pay a very high honorarium and give optimum security. In the latter case, it will, i.e. the U.S Government, provide a new identity for that person, housing, money, and a good job, including a university professorship if it becomes necessary."

"We need a spy that the U.S. and China can both run in the field," said Matt. "For the U.S., we can obtain necessary information and pass disinformation back to the Chinese. We have a potential candidate. We can change this, of course. I am going to ask Harp, who is Wuan Singh's mountain climbing buddy to approach Wuan with the proposition. The Chinese are looking for a spy (on the U.S.) to find out what we are doing with space aircraft. We have seen traces of this from our Intelligence service. At the moment, Harp and I are the only ones with anything to do on the mission. He will contact Wuan and I will work on the disinformation, logistics, and providing total security to our assistant – namely Wuan Singh."

"Are there any questions that I can answer?" asked Matt, "Otherwise, let's have a nice kick-off dinner – that is, if Kimberly has a sitter."

"She does," said Harp.

The dinner was great and Harp and Kimberly were good hosts, even though Matt was taking care of the tab for the U.S. government.

The next day, Harp and Wuan headed up the Matterhorn in Switzerland. Matt called the General to get some traction in the disinformation part of the plan.

* * *

Matt called the General on his satellite phone, and the General answered on the fifth ring that surprised Matt.

"Are you all right?" asked Matt. "You usually answer in two rings."

"I've been busy with Clark and the President," answered the General. "They are excessively worked up on the Chinese question. I suspect it is related to the country's – that is our country – security plans for the next decade. Why did you call?"

"We have plans for the Chinese affair," said Matt. "We can use a double spy – for the Chinese and for us. Both of us will run him in the field. He will obtain information for our use and pass disinformation to the Chinese."

"Sounds good if you can do it," answered the General. "Where do you get the spy?"

"There is a Chinese professor at ETH that is a climbing buddy of Harp Thomas," said Matt. "You remember Harp and his beautiful wife Kimberly."

"How can I forget them?"

"This professor, who's name is Wuan Singh, has been approached by the Chinese government to spy on America," said Matt. "Harp will asked him on a climbing trip if he would be interested in being a double spy with us guaranteeing his security. Actually, they should be climbing while we speak. Wuan's father is in the U.S. and apparently has some allegiance to us. I'm going to work on the disinformation. I would propose something facetious from something like undersee warfare."

"Sounds good to me," replied the General. "As long as we solve the open item that is what are they really doing in the area of space flight. They lie like skunks. There are no restrictions on how we do it."

"Okay, I am going to hang up now," said Matt. "Thanks for your comments."

* * *

The Matterhorn climb was routine for the experienced climbers, and Harp was back around 5 pm. He called Matt, who was staying with the team, except for the General and Anna, at the hotel Storchen and left a message. Matt called back, and they arranged a beer at the James Joyce pub, across the street from UBS, Switzerland's largest bank. Matt asked Ashley to write a disinformation piece, the gist of which was that the U.S. military was getting out of space technology because of global warming. The U.S. was moving to underwater technology. Convenient submarines – called *Subcraft* – had already been built, as well as command posts and military housing. It was a new and unexplored approach to the exploration of military technology.

Matt met Harp at the James Joyce. Harp had a Feldschlösen Premium and Matt ordered O'doul's, an American non-alcoholic beverage. Harp and Matt were PhD buddies. Harp laughed and said, "Old habits never die. Matt said, "It seems like yesterday that we studied for two years in that PhD program."

Harp was optimistic and said that Wuan Singh would be pleased to be an informant for the United States, Wuan's father lived in the states, and Wuan wished that someday he would become an American. Matt mentioned that he would be a double agent. Subsequently, Harp mentioned the double spy philosophy, and that Wuan would pass on false information to China in return for information on a particular subject important to the U.S. Wuan said being a double agent would be satisfactory to him and asked who his boss using U.S. terminology would be. Harp said that he would be his interface. He – Wuan Singh – would be given information about American military plans for the next 5 years. Harp further mentioned the source would be an earlier associate of Wuan's who was a *Nonper*, an identity without a person. Harp stated further that the U.S. contact had the name Alan Taylor in Cambridge, Massachusetts. Wuan mentioned that he had a friend at M.I.T. with that name, but Harp said there was no connection. Matt thought there was some problem therein but Harp emphasized the fact that the decision was already made. Wuan was concerned with the money, because he would like to build a house for his father in Munster, Indiana. Harp said he would be paid $1 million U.S. dollars tax free to a numbered account, and his security would be protected by the United States. It was anticipate that Wuan would meet with Chinese officials in the defense department to obtain information on hypersonic space planes that would also serve a surveillance aircraft as as well military aircraft. Further, Wuan was to initiate the operation by accepting the Chinese offer to be a spy against the United States. The

Chinese government would take care of transportation and housing for Wuan's work for the their government.

* * *

The General wanted to spend some time in Klosters, but Anna convinced him that her new teaching program was in a critical stage and she wanted to go back to the states as soon as possible. The General was angry – very angry that she hadn't informed him of her plans. Since the team was in Switzerland for bone fide mission, tha General decided to reserve the Gulfstream for the job and took a commercial flight home.

Matt was concerned with the *Nonper* named Alan Taylor, but Harp and Kimberly Scott convinced him that it was a coincidence and would have no consequence to the stated mission. Matt acquiesed.

END OF CHAPTER THIRTEEN

Chapter 14
The General's Problem

Ashley and Matt arrived home after a frustrating trip from Switzerland and looked forward to some peace and quiet, a good movie, and a bowl of popcorn.

The popcorn had just finished popping when the home phone rang. "Mr. Miller, this is New Jersey Hospital," said an office worker. "Do you know or are you related to Les Miller, one of our patients?"

"I am," said Matt. "Do you know what happened?"

"I do," said the office worker. "I am not permitted to talk, Sir, but I can assure you it is not a life or death situation."

"Thanks," said Matt. "We've been out of town, but will come to the hospital as soon as possible. In fact, we will come immediately."

Matt stood up. He had the look of someone totally exhausted. "It's always something," he said. "The General is in the hospital."

"Would you like me to come?" asked Ashley.

"You do not have to," replied Matt. "I would appreciate it if you did."

The New Jersey General Hospital was just a few minutes away, and Matt parked in the 'No Parking' area in front of the entrance.

"This is no parking," said Ashley.

"I don't care," said Matt. "Let them fine me."

Wearing their face masks, Ashley and Matt went to registration and up to the General's room, numbered 441.

"Hi Matt," said the General. "Thank you for coming."

"What happened General?" asked Matt.

"I slipped on some wet pavement stepping over the curb, and fell on the left side of my left knee. It's the one that had a knee replacement after making a dead-stick landing in a P-51. I was afraid that I had damaged the knee post-thesis, but it turned out to be a vertical beak in the bone just above the knee. They call it a fractured femur. The surgeon put in a vertical piece of metal and screwed it to my femur. Actually, it doesn't hurt very much and I have to go to physical therapy (PT) and occupational therapy (OT) starting tomorrow. I'm not allowed to put weight on the bone and learn how to take a shower. Actually, I had one yesterday."

"I bet that was a pleasure," said Matt.

"I have six weeks of rehab," mentioned the General.

"Does that mean you will be up and walking in six weeks?" asked Matt.

"Not exactly," replied the General. "They will take an X-ray and if all is okay, I will start walking therapy. The doctor said that the femur is the slowest bone to heal in the whole body."

"Why didn't you go to the military hospital in DC?" continued Matt.

The doctor said it would take too long to make the connection and then geet there," said Matt. This is a good hospital, and they are nice to the patients here.

"Are you eating good?" asked Ashley.

"The food is really excellent, but I'm just not hungry. They give me a protein drink every day that I really dislike. I can't stand it. I'd like a sip of single malt scotch."

"You're not likely to get it here," said Ashley with a smile.

"I'm just talking," replied the General. "There is no one to talk to around here. They wake me up every hour or so for something or another. I have to take 1000 mg of vitamin D and get an iron transfusion every day. The latter because there is a blood shortage in the States, caused by the pandemic – so they say."

"We've got to go," said Matt. "We just got back from Switzerland on that China project. We are exhausted."

"How did it turn out?" asked the General.

"The final answer is that the China does not have any aircraft like our V-37 hypersonic space machine. They were just bluffing. Our double spy, Wuan Singh, got the result we were after, but he and his mole are in big trouble. I think their cover was blown. I'll tell you when we ge the final answer. It's messy and we said we would protect our spy. I'll fill you in when I hear how thinks are progressing. We have a Russian faculty member that could possibly help us. I'll let you know about this also. It looks like we will have to go back to Europe to take care of things. Is it okay to use the Gulfstream?"

"Yes, by all means," answered the General. "Let me know when we can give the final result to Mark Clark and then to the President."

"I think we will have the result and the final resolution in about 4 days," said Matt. I can't be exact, since there are several open items."

Matt stepped out for a few minutes, and when he returned, he said he had some information on the General's expected progress.

"You'll be in here for two more weeks and then home for 4 weeks until your leg mends," said Matt. "The nurse said you will have specific physical and occupational therapy. When they say you're done, you are done, and not before. This is definitely not my specialty and my interests do not lie here. One of us will here every day to see how you are progressing."

"I'll be here," said the General. "Thanks for the visit.'

* * *

On the way home, Ashley volunteered to visit the General every day and play backgammon or something like that. Matt agreed and said he would get started on a report and third and final project.

"You know," said Matt. "I'm totally tired of traveling, meting, swards, and so forth. I'm so looking forward to being an ordinary professor again, like I used to be."

"Some people thrive on it," replied Ashley. "I personally look back at our first coffee together at Starbucks. To me, you were amazing and knew about everything and could do everything."

"I thought that of you, also," said Matt.

The next day, Ashley brought her portable backgammon set to the hospital and the General refused to learn the game or even try to play it. All the General would do is to grumble about how dull the hospital is and when he could get out of there. The next day, the nurse brought in a retrofitted computer named the MacBook Air. She told the General she had received it from her son who said it was turned in on the new model. She gave the used computer to the General.

"What should I do with it?" asked the General.

"Well, you could play games or write yourself a letter, like the famous song, or ever write a story," said the nurse. "Can you use a word processor? She asked.

"Of course I can," said the General. "How stupid do you think I am?"

"Just give it a try," said the Nurse. If you don't like it, I'll give it back."

The next morning when the nurse came in to the General's room. He was beaming like a little kid.

"What happened to you," she said. "You are a new man."

The General opened the MacBook and said, "Look at this. What do you think?"

The General displayed the following essay on the screen.

<u>A Smile</u>

I was heading down Atlantic Avenue in Boston to the office buildig where I work. It was noontime and the sidewalk was filled with people. As I walked, I was eating a candy bar. I don't even remember why and what kind it was. I approached a nice looking young women, who had a huge smile on her face. At the time I thought the smile was because of the candy bar that I as eating. The smile started at a distance and lasted until we passed each other. I have a lingering memory of that event. It made me feel good – a simple smile. What was it about a smile that would make a person – namely me - remember the episode? What is a smile anyway?

A smile is a facial expression accomplished by opening one's mouth slightly or minimally showing the teeth and flexing the lips. A smile may be seen in the twinkle of the eyes. In the latter case it is called a Duchine smile. The word smile is derived from the middle English word Smilen. There a lot of sayings that include the word smile, such as people commonly say, "Smile and people smile with you; frown and you frown alone." Actually, there are two forms if the word smile. There is the noun representing the smile itself, and the verb form that is the act of smiling and called the previously mentioned Dushine smile. There are two substitutes for the word smile: beam and grin. For example, the boy received a bicycle for Christmas and he was beaming. Alternately, the word grin is more common, as in George has a foolish grin on his face after telling a joke.

* * *

"That is terrific," said the nurse. "Is it finished?"

"Not yet," replied the General. My wife a former writing professor, and she says I have a talent as a writer. My grandson Matt says it is the way I express myself."

"The general showed his work to Matt whe he came in.

"Sir, that is terrific," said Matt with a smile.

The next morning, Matt came to the hospital early, surprising the General.

"You're up so something." said the General.

"I tried my hand at writing last night," said Matt. "It probably isn't a good as yours. "I printed my copy."

Here is what he wrote:

The Window

Now why would anyone write about one of the most common things in the modern world: a window. After all, there are windows all over the place, and many of them don't have anything covering them up. Probably, there is an interest in windows – especially open ones – because there is almost always a sort of mystery associated with a window. There is natural inclination to find out what's going on. Is it something new and challenging, is it something drastic, is it something that is exceedingly happy or terribly sad?

Try to conceptualize strolling in the country side and coming upon an older building with blown out open windows, what is the first thing you think? Probably it is that no one cares. But that is not necessarily true. Perhaps the owner has passed away and just does not know that the beloved structure with damaged windows is in need of repair. Does caring end with death? Well, that is an open item. It seems that life in the modern world is nothing more than an ever expanding set of open items. Back to the wide world of windows.

It is entirely possible that there were never any covers of any kind over the rectangular "holes in a proverbial wall". The place was simply not finished, a commonplace consequence for a variety of everyday reasons. What about the windows in some of those middle-eastern homes. It seems as though they typically don't have anything covering the windows – at least that's how they are portrayed in the daily news.

Probably it is easier to shoot through an open window and even an open door. That pertains to inside out and is likely true of outside in.

* * *

That is really good," said the General. You're much better than I am."

"I doubt it," said Matt. "I think we're equal. It was a lot of fun. Ashley said that I hadn't been so pleased in a long time. I think writing is relaxing.

END OF CHAPTER FOURTEEN

Chapter 15
The Escape

In the fifth day, the General received a text message from Matt stating that the mission had been completed successfully and a report would arrive the next day. Matt would be home on the seventh day. There was no good news, other than what was expected and no bad news.

Ashley and Matt returned on the seventh day – a one week mission. Actually, end-to-end it was longer but no one counted those things. It was quite a job and one of which the U.S. could be proud. Matt had done an impressive task of pulling the details together and effectively preserved the sanctity of an American operation. Matt started the session.

"Everything is okay," said Matt. "There were some uncertain events that we had to take care of. The Chinese government provided a first-class ticket for Wuan Singh's travel to Beijing and gave him a lot of money for expenses. He was pleased. He was ordered to check in to an expensive hotel and report to an overall strategy meeting the next day in a suburb of Beijing. Wuan got to meet a lot of top military officers in the meeting and showed his outgoing personality to obtain the information we wanted him to obtain. Wuan managed to sneak in a question about hypersonic aircraft and found that the Chinese have nothing other than wishful thinking. All of their big talk was pure propaganda. Wuan relayed the disinformation on what the U.S. was doing in the area of undersea warfare and that did not appear to raise any eyebrows. Wuan noted that the Chinese miliary establishment had overall acceptance over what they were doing to impress the country of Taiwan – whatever that is. The military leader asked how he obtained his information and Wuan told about his former associate that was actually the *Nonper* at M.I.T. Apparently, there is someone there with the same name. That was an error on the U.S. intelligence service. They checked on the *Nonper* and that was where the truth came out. The *Nonper*'s name is Alan Taylor and apparently, there is a person at M.I.T. with that name. The first night, our mole approached Wuang and told him they were in trouble, including the mole himself. We never heard the name of the mole, for security reasons. The *Nonper* was handled by Kimberly Scott and apparently someone screwed up, and at that point, it was too late to change. All the mole said to Wuan was, "We have to get out of here. They found out the source did not exist. We have to leave immediately. The authorities usually start their work just before dawn, and they are probably headed our way. I have Yak-152 that I use for recreation. It's a very old Russian plane that people here and in Russia use for recreation. Leave all personal belongs behind. This is a matter of life or death."

"I received only one message from Wuan," said Matt. "He said they were headed across the Bering sea and would land in a deserted Russian airport named Folding Airport"

That was when I went into action. A good Russian friend of mine Alexi Belov, that I brought into the U.S. and to our math department has a dynamic father in Russia who likes to make money – especially dollars – and owns another of those old Yal-152 and said he could pick up the mole and Wuan and bring them to the deserted military airport that we used just tnorth of Moscow. He said he needed $1 million and I accepted his offer. He brought his cargo, namely Wuan and the mole, to the old military airport. When he arrived, we were already there. I offered to bring the human cargo to the States, but they wanted to return to Zürich. I said they were crazy as loons, but they insisted. They said the Swiss government had kicked all Chinese out of Switzerland. They insisted so Ashley and I returned to the states in the Gulfstream, and here we are. Safe and sound. By the way, I forced a cool $1 million on my friend Alexi Belov. The total operation was expensive to the country but well worth the cost. To sum up, we got the information we wanted, and our disinformation concerning undersea operations is an open item. Who knows.

Lastly, I think Wuan and his mole are a bit too daring, and we probably will not see or hear about them again. Ashley will summarize our events and the second problem has been resolved.

The General said, "Thank you and the country thanks you."

END OF CHAPTER FIFTEEN AND PART II

Part III
The Final Project

Chapter 16
Presidential Visit to the General

The bad news came a couple of days later. Matt came to the hospital ealier than usual and ran into a nurse in the hallway leading to the General's room – number 441. All she said was, "The General is going to be with us for about 3 more weeks. He has to go through Physical and Occupational Therapy before we allow him to join the outside world. The actual date is written on the white board in his room. Then he needs at-home physical therapy. At first he was furious, but when the Hospitalist, who is a very persuasive young women came to talk to him, he quieted down and accepted the situation. Then a small jet plane landed on the hospital runway, and a couple of important looking young men dashed into the building, spent no more than 10 minutes inside, and then left without even turning off the plane. Most of the staff did not even know they were here. Then the director came around and shouted, which was strange for him, "Clean this place up immediately and look your best. We have an important visitor at noon. No questions, just snap to it."

Matt walked to room 441, and the General was propped up in his bed with a half eaten breakfast on the tray. "Good morning Matt," said the General. "it's good to see you. Something big is going to happen and we have to be in ship shape."

"The nurse just told me," replied Matt. "Do you know what's going on?"

"No," said the General, "but the Hospitalist came back

in and supervised as a nurse and a steward put the room in perfect shape. Sounds bad to me."

"Quite the opposite," said Matt. "They only clean the place up for good news."

* * *

At 11:00 sharp, a group of men and women in official business dress came in. Every room had someone in front of it. A tough looking guy came in to the General's room and directed a curt question at Matt.

"Where's Ashley?" he said.

"She's at home," said Matt.

"Get her!" said the man to an associate, "and on the double. Use blue lights and we'll alert the city police while you're at it."

Fifteen minutes later, Ashley walked in the door. She quickly ran over to Matt, and asked, "What's going on?"

All Matt could do was shrug his shoulders. They looked at the General. He was calm, as one might expect as an experienced fighter pilot.

At 11:45, in walked President Kenneth Strong and along with him was his wife Elizabeth. The President shook the General's hand and his wife gave Matt a big hug. They were friends.

"General, you and your team are the best. I'm here to give you and each of your team, that is, Matt and Ashley, the highest civilian award, the Medal of Freedom. Second, we need a record of your relevant activities for the government archive. I will be leaving presidential office soon, so it has to be done as soon as possible. I would like it to be a person-to-person discussion. Here's what that means to the government. We do not care about literary details, such as structure, references, spelling, quotation marks, and spelling. We want facts only. We want the report for each of the projects you have performed, described to me as though we were having a conversation and you were having a discussion with me. The third project, concerning the pandemic, is well documented and any further work on it is not required. We need definitive information on each of the projects the team has performed on the behalf of the country. The third project is now a definitive description on all of those projects. The conditions remain the same. Your personal judgment may be required in some cases, and in some instances the events presented need not be specific to the governement"

The President continued. "There is another consideration. You, the General, Matt, and Ashley have become more well-known than we ever imagined. Too many people know you and of you. It's time for a rest.

The awards were presented forthwith and the President and staff left. In 10 minutes, the hospital staff was back in action.

END OF CHAPTER SIXTEEN

Chapter 17
The People in the Archive Report

The primary persons involved in the archive are Matt Miller, Les (the General) Miller, who is Matt's grandfather, Ashley Wilson Miller, Matt's wife, and Charles (Buzz) Bunday, who is the General's Army buddy. They are the primary characters in the activities of the General's team. There are other people. Who might the leader be? Of course, who else would the leader, other than the person named the General.

Here is a snapshot of exactly whom we are talking about. The snapshot includes Lt. Buzz Bunday, the General's wing man, and the Air Force commander. They are waiting for Lt. Les Miller to return from his flight in a new U.S. fighter plane known as the P-51. As the saying goes, if you have a P-51 on your tail, you're a goner. The fighters normally accompany and protect bombers, such as the B-17, who are on a mission. Miller is on the tail of a German fighter plane that shot down an Allied bomber. Buzz told Miller to forget the enemy because he might use up his fuel. The commander said, "He's either run out of fuel or got shot down." Buzz, who is Miller's buddy replied, "Let's give him a few more minutes." The commander answered, "You've got 2 minutes. I've got work to do." "I hear something," said Buzz. "It sounds like a 51. It's him." The commander replied, "His engine just shut off, must be he's out of fuel." Les Miller, the General, makes a dead stick landing and runs into a barrier, put up for that purpose. The General jumps out of his P-51, trips, wrenches his knee, and says, "I got him, he's a goner. That is 36 kills for me." The commander turns and says that the two lieutenants should report to him in the morning at 8:00. The two pilots have completed the Air Force requirement of 25 sorties. In the commander's office at 8:00 the next morning, the pilots enter and salute the commander. "At ease gentlemen," says the commander. "By my records, you have completed your Air Force requirement of 25 flights. Attention! You are now promoted to the rank of Captain, U.S. Army Air Force., with all rights and privileges pertaining thereto. In your case Bunday, you have the British equivalent. You have two weeks leave in the states and then ordered to report to the Pentagon. You're expenses are covered by the government. Good luck." That was the end of World War II combat for the General and Buzz.

At the Pentagon, Captain Miller and Captain Bunday were ordered to report to a high level secret meeting about the number of P-51s or other fighters that are shot down in one mission: as many as 60% per mission. The Air Force tried titanium panels and the method didn't work. The meeting is being attended by three-star generals, college professors, and noted scientists. They laugh when the Captains are introduced. "What good are a couple of Captains when the smartest men in the country cannot solve the problem." The problem is defined. All of the bullet holes are covered up but the planes continue to be shot down. Captain Les Miller says, "I can solve the problem." The others just laugh and take a coffee break. Buzz says, "Les, are you out of your mind? You're probably going to get demoted."

When the meeting got going again, Captain Miller was asked to describe the method that he says will solve the problem. Here is Miller's response. "The objective of the meeting is to determine where titanium plates are to be placed for protection of P-51s. Here are some photos." The photos showed P-51s with bullet holes. "The planes have been plated where the holes are with no improvement. Now, here is why we are here. It's an easy problem." The rest of the audience just laughed and looked each other. They thought that was why they were there, to solve the problem. Miller is off his rocker.

Captain Miller continued, "It's easy gentlemen. The important holes went down with the plane – in fact, probably caused it. Look at the photos, do you see any planes with holes in the bellies, for example. Armor plate the untouched areas and the problem will be solved." Note: the armor plating was placed in clean aircraft bellies, and the percent of shot down planes was reduced to 10%. This is a true story. Captain Miller, and his buddy Bunday were promoted forthwith to Major. Again, this is a true story. The author has researched it and read the descriptive math paper that describes it. It was termed reverse mathematics.

There is one more description of the General. As is commonly the case, if an Army officer deserves promotion but there is no open slot, he or she must retire. That is the case of General Les Miller. He had several interesting episodes, such as landing a transport plane, filled with officers and also generals, where the pilot and co-pilot were disabled. He was forced to retire as a three-star. Once out, he happened to call his friend Bill Donovan from the Nuremburg war trials. Donovan became President of Pratt Institute in Brooklyn New York. In fact, the author had an office in his building. Donovan said to General Miller, "I was once in your position Les, why don't you come to Pratt and get an M.S. in computer Science?" The General did just that, getting his MS and meeting some Iranians, one of which is portrayed in Chapter 10 of this book. So much for the General. Next are Dr. Matt Miller and Ashley.

Matt and Ashley were college friends. They met is a college writing course and met casually at Starbucks and the library. Matt was a college golf champion and Ashley was a practicing drama student. That means she was in some plays. Matt was a dedicated student who possessed an exceptional amount of common sense. Ashley was interested in becoming a noteworthy actress, eventually marrying an English Prince. Make graduated with a PhD in math and started a successful academic career in the distinguished university from which he obtained his first degree.

Buzz Bunday was indeed an unusual person. He was an excellent student with an overload of good common sense. He was a member of the English Air Force who was cooperating with the U.S. Air Force. After leaving the Air Force, Buzz joined the British Security Service, where he became a chief officer. He was well-known in English circles and was regarded as a person who could get things done. He was awarded a knighthood in the Royal Kingdom and was henceforth known as Sir Charles Bunday. Sir Charles was a powerful asset to the General's team.

There were several others who worked with the General's, most notably was Dr. Marguerite Purgoine, Matt and Ashley's writing professor. Dr. Purgoine, who was known as Anna for some unknown reason, married the General and became a valuable member of the team.

END OF CHAPTER SEVENTEEN

Chapter 18
The Archive Report

The archival data is arranged chronologically. The personage in the report is described in the accompanying documentation.

The Royal Baby

Through careful planning and a little bit of luck, Ashley made her way to the top of the social mountain. She and Prince Michael, the grandson of the Queen of England, were married in a glamorous English ceremony. The groom was handsome and the bride was glamorous. She was a beautiful starlet with all of the intellect pertaining thereto. As usual, the first question asked by the English media was when was she going to have a baby. It was the tradition among royalty marriages. Ashley was in a panic. She absolutely did not want to lose her movie-star figure.

What does one do when faced with a seemingly insoluble problem? Contact Matt. Oh, there is one more problem. Ashley is biracial – at least she thinks she is. The British media would have a field day if her ethnicity ever came out. A white couple with an African American baby would be more than the English people could stand. The English media would go crazy.

Ashley contacts Matt via the messaging system and they agree on a surrogate baby, even to the extent that the sperm should be British. Matt goes to the General and they work out an ingenious plan to obtain a surrogate baby and its nanny. One of the candidates for the position of nanny makes the statement that she would like to spy for the Americans. Of course, she is not selected but Ashley makes an innocuous remark that being a spy would be interesting. Nothing materializes in that regard.

The General proposes to use his private Gulfstream G650, paid for with personal funds, and arranges with Buzz Bunday to land with the baby in a private airport north of London. Ashley uses a pad in her abdomen to emulate her baby bump. The surrogate baby is transferred to Michael and Ashley and all seems to be satisfactory.

The Queen is a wise women and makes friends with the nanny. She uses the age-old trick of giving a little bit of information to get a lot. The nanny just mentions the spy incident, which had been forgotten.

The nanny has a free day every Saturday and is strolling about to enjoy the day. She crosses a London street and looks the wrong way. She is hit by a taxi and later dies in the hospital.

The General says to Matt, "Matt, we preserved the sanctity of the royal family line. We should be saddened and proud. We did our job. Case closed." Reference: Katzan, H., *The Mysterious Case of the Royal Baby.*

The Royal Marriage

Prince Michael and Ashley were given the titles of Duke and Duchess of Bordeaux and their baby was named Philip George William Charles and referred to as Master Philip. They were given the property known as Malbec outside of the domain of the palace. Ashley was unhappy over the royal requirements and asked Michael for a divorce.

Michael informed her that a wife was under the control of her husband in the Monarchy and only he could grant a divorce, which in this case he would not do so. Marriage rules of royalty were outside of the scope of traditional English and American marriage conventions. Marriage licenses, driver's licenses, birth certificates, and passports were all handled specially.

Ashley said to Michael that she didn't know what to do and who to consult for advice. Ironically, Michael referred to Matt. Ashley wrote in her personal diary that she didn't even want the baby, probably because she knew it was a surrogate baby.

Ashley sent a message to Matt and they discussed the situation. Matt was surprised at the complications of being a royal and said he would discuss the situation with the General, who knew Ashley and liked her.

Matt and the General discussed Ashley's situation and surmised that Ashley's life would probably be in danger, and she would have to be extracted. The fact that Ashley was in constant surveillance was a major consideration. They would have to call upon Sir Charles for assistance. The General explained the problem and Buzz said they had similar requirements in the past. Buzz proposed the following scenario: "You should stage a suicide. The person in danger should jump off the London bridge and never be found. This takes her or she off the books – so to speak. We can have a frogman portray the person involved and swim to the shore without being observed. Here is how it should be planned. We might as well speak of the person involved by her real name. There are no secrets around here. There are security cameras everywhere in London. The General asked how it would work if there were followers. Buzz said they could take care of that. There are security cameras, except behind the Scotland Yard building and the windows are blackened so people can't see in. Ashley will stop behind the Scotland Yard building and an accident will be staged so the follower can't see her. Ashley will leave her car – we see the Michael has given her a new Jaguar – with the engine running and go to the black car that will take here to a safe house. The frogman will drive her car in plain sight, stop, and jump into the water. He will be dressed the same as Ashley, so that observers will think it is she, effectively exiting a suicide The safe house is a hotel, the upper floor of which are used by the BSS. Buzz stated that thhe rest of the extraction operation was up to Matt and the General.

Matt and the General planned a military entrance into the United States with Matt and Ashley dressed as Lt. Colonel and Captain, respectively. Uniforms, ID cards, and passports will be provided. Matt and Ashley changed clothes and an agent transported them to the London City Airport where the Gulfstream G650 was waiting. The General stayed at home in the states for the total operation. Military officers are treated with respect and usually enter the states with no difficulty. That was the case with Matt and Ashley. Their flight landed in the U.S. and the Matt and Ashley were transported to the General's home. Ashley was afforded a face modification, a name change, and a good U.S. business position.

The extraction was performed with no expense to the government. Reference: Katzan, H., *The Curious Case of the Royal Marriage.*

The General and the Royal Family

One of the things that the General always wanted to do was to pilot a B52 bomber. The General always said that piloting a fighter plane was like driving a sports car, and piloting a large bomber was like driving a large Mercedes. Les Miller, the General, got his chance. Someone with a high rank and an outstanding record was need to fly a B52 to Area 51, the government's secret research facility in Nevada. The guess was that the B52 would be used to carry an air craft to predetermined height and from then on let the craft fly itself using artificial intelligence for navigation. He needed two weeks of training and flew the B52 to Area 51. He flew directly to the secret area and immediately was directed to small plane for return to Las Vegas. He got his wish.

The General's assistant, Dr. Matt Miller was an accomplished scientist. He with an associate who was an geneticist, analyzed a sample of Ashley's DNA and determined that Ashley was not biracial but singly Caucasian. At the time Ashley was going under the name Sara Nicole Harris. She was adopted a biracial who raised her as a biracial child with all of its advantages and disadvantages. Moreover, Ashley and Prince Michael were not legally married but united by royal decree with no legal value. Ashley Wilson would become a valuable member of the General's team.

A Case of Espionage

Matt and the General combine their efforts to solve a murder mystery that involves a research project at a major university. The leader of the project, the Dean of

Engineering, is murdered and the administration cannot come up with a solution. A professor is suspected.

Matt and the General uncover a solution through the British Monarchy, a professor of physics from England, and the efforts of a four-star U.S. General. A key scientist and his wife are extracted from England through a bit of trickery and use the General's plane to escape from England.

Shelter in Place

The *Shelter* is an unusual combination of the pandemic, academics, and the military to thwart an attempt to assassinate the president, in a contest of the United States, England, and Switzerland.

This is the first instance of Matt in the series in an official position. Matt had done a little, but he had not been able to use his keen intellect to assist in solving real-life problems, which in fact is, in this case, the assassination of the President of the United States of America. Matt, whose complete name is Dr. Matthew Miller, is a professor of mathematics in a prestigious university. The math professor involved with the problem sent Matt a message asking his assistance. Matt called the General who knew a language expert, who thought it was, in fact, a valid problem. The language expert named Allan Weinberg verified the suspicion and the government took care of the situation. An assassination of the President had been averted.

This is the first time in the context in of the book where Matt has dealt with beautiful women while acting las an investigative scientist.

Matt and the General travel with their team to investigate the notice that the free world is in danger.

The danger to the world would take three avenues: the worldwide oil industry, the German automobile industry, and the British royalty. Their work was complete. They identified the worldwide threats and were free to address the situation at the newly founded astrophysics lab. Matt's publishing protégé was accepted as the admin at the lab.

It was determined that the suspicious terrorism events were in fact outsourced. The pandemic was the primary danger, and its source has not been absolutely determined.

The Virus

The COVID-19 virus made a tremendous impact on the world. In short, it is a plague. Here is a summary:

- The virus is referred to as a coronavirus.
- The first outbreak was in China in the year 2020.
- The virus spread quickly. In a few months it was worldwide.
- The transmission had been person-person.
- The origin is not clear.
- The symptoms a high temperature, dry cough, and fatigue.
- 80% of affected persons recover without medical treatment.
- There is no vaccine or treatment.
- The virus affected older people most readily.
- Incubation is 1 to 14 days.
- Precautions are face mask, social distancing, and hand washing.
- The "stay home" motto has been affective.

- Social gatherings and restaurant have been forced to close.
- The U.S. government has paid a supplement as taxpayers.
- Commodities have been hoarded.
- No effort has been made to determine the source of the virus.

There are many theories on the origin of the virus. Bats are a common source but not verified. Out of space is another mention. One promising idea is that countries that limit the number of children to one is the source since they may desire to limit worldwide population. China is a likely example. There are only a few realistic subjects that are listed as options.:

- Initial transmission between persons.
- Worldwide travel.
- Politics of virus protection.
- Origin of the virus.
- Techniques for harm reduction.

Harm reduction refers to public health tools and practices – such as needle exchange programs or safe sex with condoms, designed to lower danger without having a total medical solution.

The U.S. desires to find out relevant answers and has arranged with the team of Matt and the General to determine answers to the above questions.

The team decoded on two teams, one for the U.S. and one for England, the leading countries engaging in virus research. The persons in the U.S. team consist of: Mme. Purgoine, Ashley Wilson, Amelia Robinson, Kimberly

Thomas, Harp Thomas, and Harry Steevens, under the direction of Dr. Matt Stevens. The English team, called the foreign team, under the direction of the General is Colonel Charles Bunday (BSS), William Bunday (BSS). And Gustav from Germany. It is intended that the teams will cooperation in determined the origin of the virus. The work is sponsored by the U.S. government.

The foreign team determined that the German viral attack was outsourced by a large amount of an unknown source. One of the U.S. methods for spreading the virus is Asymptomatic Transmission, where persons with no symptoms spread the virus. Typical examples are beaches and school. A 100 million dollar transmission of money was discovered verifying, somewhat, the concept of outsourcing. The notion that the virus came from outer space surfaced at this stage of the investigation.

The Pandemic

Here is a description of a pandemic. An *endemic* is sickness that belongs to a particular people or country. An *outbreak* is a greater-than-anticipated increase in the number of endemic cases. Of an outbreak is not controlled, it is call an *epidemic*. Lastly, a *pandemic* is an epidemic that spreads over multiple countries or continents and affects a large number of people. The sequence is: *endemic > outbreak > epidemic > pandemic.* The two main concerns are the source and how to identify it, cure it, and prevent it.

Matt and the General were called to provide pandemic data for the state of the union address, the next election, and a report to the nation. They would be working with a Presidential associate. The project is top secret – not the information, but the fact that the President is interested in it.

The situation is complicated, since the presidential associate is regarded as a Russian spy, called a mole, and then it is found to be a spy for the U.S. That is the case in *Pandemic.*

The designer of the virus, as it turns out, was a Russian neuroscientist who intended to develop the virus and the antidote and receive the Noble prize. As it turns out, he died, of the virus, before the antidote was completed.

Life is good

Matt started off the excitement by investigating the disappearance of the President's wife which is a strange thing to happen in the White House. The President knows that if the cat gets out of the bag, it will result in worldwide attention of a negative proportion. Matt and the General are called into action by the existing President, First of all, Dr. Matt Miller was award the Outstanding Scholar award by his university followed by an interesting trip to Maui for a vacation.

The context for the event is as interesting as the event itself. The existing President, Kenneth String whose wife's name is Elizabet, was in a fast trip to the west coast to visit an old friend and associate who was on his death bed. They had a long standing pledge to the effect that one would be with the other. On the way, the General and his team are then headed to Maui. The General's Gulfstream is headed to Maui at full speed by retired F-22 pilots. Their path comes close to the President's Air Force One and some military jets were scrambled to protect him. Recall that such as episode would have taken place at long distances such as 10 to 20 miles. The pilot's converse and all is well. The President returns and it is late in the evening. The President does not want to wake his wife who has a case of the flu. The next morning, he awakens to find his wife has disappeared. An exhaustive search comes up with nothing in the capital city and elsewhere. Everything is on the QT. Matt and the General are called.

The White House is again searched and the select service, a synonym for the secret service, again finds nothing. Matt determines they are looking in the wrong place. They are looking where she is supposed to be and should be looking where she is not supposed to be. They eventually uncover some wartime cells in a tunnel between the White House and an adjacent government building. The key are long lost. The Army Core of Engineers opens the first cell and they find nothing. They determine they are wasting their time. Matt says, "Look at the hand grips soiled by 50 years of dust and dirt. Look at one wherein the grim and dirt are not present." The Army Core opens the door and viola, there are the President's wife and her select service agent. Matt asked how they got in there, and the agent says he was in charge during the war and saved the key. "Why did you assist Mrs. Strong?" The agent replies that he was ordered to do whatever the First Lady asked hm to do. The First Lady was embarrassed because she looked so poorly because of the flu. The angry President was summoned and Matt advised him as follows, "Be kind to her, Mr. President, she needs you now."

This event is important because it sets the stage for the "Vaccine" and the "Pandemic." First, the origin of the virus was of some interest. Natural sources and man-made being the top two options. Method for combining alternate sources was developed in this period.

During this period, Matt developed a theory of the pandemic that is delineated in the following paragraphs.

It turns that pathogens are spread in clusters, such that some individuals having the disease can spread it more than others, who spread it less frequently. It explains why a small region in Italy had an enormous death toll from COVID-19, and other regions had very few or none at all. It's analogous to the 80/20 rule that seems to guide the use of computer software. Many studies use the subject of averages, but that doesn't necessarily apply. Take a drinking bar for example. If you take the average income of all customers, you get some relatively small number. If Jeff Bezos or Bill Gates then walks in, the average is much higher. For example, some large groups of infected people do not infect a single other person, whereas a very small group, say one person, can infect many others. In Hong Kong, 19 percent of cases were responsible for 89 percent of transmissions, while 69 percent of cases did not infect another person. The subject matter is called Evolutionary Biology, and the phenomena is referred to as dispersion, or sometimes referred to as over-dispersion.

The Vaccine

Matt, Ashley, and the General were curious about the status of the COVID-19 virus and decided to find out what was going on by visiting Mark Clark, former Chairman of the Joint Chiefs of Staff at the Pentagon. Clark was unusually tight lipped on the subject and the conversation centered primarily what preventative would be required of the military troops. Onn the way home, the team decided to go it alone and investigate the matter.

Pursuant to a math conference in Zürich, Matt made contacts to mathematical friends and decided to use the math department as an entry into Russian research. The contacts proved useful and a Russian virologist was identified. He was invited to the states and eventually made director of a virology lab in southern Ohio. The President of the university, an associate of the President of the United States, facilitated the total operation. The Russian sources were productive and provided valuable results.

Some of the areas of interest in the reports include the following:

- Introduction and overview
- What is a virus?
- How am virus spreads
- UK coronavirus variant
- How do COVID-19 vaccines work
- Unfortunate destinations
- Herd immunity
- Operation warp speed
- Side effects of the vaccines
- Distribution costs
- How a vaccine works
- Vaccine storage
- mRNA: Pfizer and Moderna
- Origin of viruses
- Activities in China
- Activities in Russia
- Allergic reaction to vaccines
- Miscellaneous comments

These are some of the most important subjects of the current generation.

A Tale of Discovery

Major events, such as a pandemic, engender a lot of basic research. For example, World War II resulted in research than would not have been performed otherwise. Discovering the origin of the COVID-19 virus is just one of those things. Bats from China and advanced developments from Russia are just wo of them. One person thinks that countries that limit the number of children per family are the culprits and are interested in keeping the birth rate of the world down. In this scenario, Matt, the team, and Prince Michael have experienced an unusual possibility. Perhaps, the COVID-19 virus has an origin from outer space.

Prince Michael had a position as director of the astrophysics in a major university. He adopted the name Michael Davis so as to not emphasize the fact that he was royalty. He did not get along well with his staff since British work habits differed from those of Americans. On one, and perhaps more than one occasion, he used the wrong instrument for the right task. He observed evidence that UFOs were coming from the Pinwheel Galaxy. As it turned out, the planet Zenex had characteristics the same a planet Earth. When Prince Michael mentioned that fact to his American colleagues, the laughed at him. He subsequently left the States and returned to the Monarchy. Matt heard of the situation and offered a unique possibility.

Mat offered the remark that, 'Why do UFOs always fly around with their lights on. If you put flashlight on a drone you get an UFO. The UFOs in the U.S. skies are up to something.' The conjecture was offered that perhaps the persons from Zenex were scouting us out because the planet Zenex was going extinct. They wanted to kill off all of the people on Earth with the virus and replace them with people from Zenex.

The people in the UFO were living in a sort of Closed Ecological System comprised of plants, fish, water, and human individuals. An American space company had experimented with a CES, but little is known about the idea. There are other considerations that may support the conclusion that the virus came from out space.

A few years age, a UFO had crashed in he southwest part of the country and the U.S. Army had taken the remains to a place in Navada now called Area 51.

There is another conjecture that the solar dust that originates in Saudi Arabia contains the virus.

This could be very interesting reading for a future scientist.

The Terrorist Plot

The Terrorist Plot is a relatively short project located in Hilton Head designed to crash a plane into the White House. It is conjectured that is was designed by bin Ladin's brother as revenge to his brother's, Osama bin Laden, elimination. Of course, the project failed and this project describes how it was averted.

There is evidence that the reputation of the team consisting of Matt, Ashley, Anna, the General, and Sir Charles Bunday, has gotten around. Most of the action in this episode is done behind the scenes.

The underlying idea about Hilton Head is that the

residents are older and trend not to be concerned about the visitors to the small community. Gangs of young men are evident and most people regard them as Hispanics. In reality, they can and are frequently Iranians. It is relatively easy to enter and reside in Hilton Head. In many cases, many families in the area are Iranian entered illegally. One practice, however, gave them away. The mothers frequently meet in the local coffee shop a after they have left their kids off in school. They chatter away in Farsi, and most residents think it is Spanish Remember, the population is older. However, one resident who knew Spanish and other languages said it is not Spanish, but Iranian Farsi. The practice filtered its way into the intelligence community and an assignment is made to General Mark Clark, the former leader of the chiefs of staff.

Through a routine game of golf, Clark enrolls the team of Matt, Ashley, Anna, and the General. The plan is to purchase unused planes from New Mexico and fly them to an unused airbase in New Hampshire. From there, they had planned to cripple the defense zone and crash into the White House. Matt, Ashley, and the General avert the plan and have the enemy planes shot down over the Atlantic ocean. The sounds are questioned by independent persons and the media and the military report they are sonic booms.

The Iranian plot is ingenious, but the team Matt, Ashley, Anna, and the General is smarter than they are.

An Untimely Situation

This section gives a brief notation of three project initiated by the White House. Accordingly, no description is required.

The first is the identity and capture of a perpetrator of

a ransomware attack on the military establishment. The Iranian spy turned out to be a person named Atalus. He was captured and turned to be a mole for the U.S. His American name is Adam Benfield.

The second project was a description of the illegal technique of ransomware wherein a criminal invades a computer system and ties up various data elements and capabilities until a ransom is paid.

The final project is thwarting of an assignation of the Director of Intelligence.

END OF CHAPTER EIGHTEEN, PART III, AND THE BOOK

Afterword

The two vignettes contained in chapter 14 were not written by the Genera and Matt because they don't exist in real life. However, the vignettes do exist and were prepared by the author. The complete items are given her for the reader's pleasure. Enjoy.

A Smile

I was heading down Atlantic Avenue in Boston to the office building where I work. It was noontime and the sidewalk was filled with people. As I walked, I was eating a candy bar. I don't even remember why and what kind it was. I approached a nice looking young women, who had a huge smile on her face. At the time I thought the smile was because of the candy bar that I as eating. The smile started at a distance and lasted until we passed each other. I have a lingering memory of that event. It made me feel good – a simple smile. What was it about a smile that would make a person – namely me - remember the episode? What is a smile anyway?

A smile is a facial expression accomplished by opening one's mouth slightly or minimally showing the teeth and flexing the lips. A smile may be seen in the twinkle of the eyes. In the latter case it is called a 'Dushine' smile. The word 'smial' is derived from the middle English word 'smilen.' There a lot of sayings that include the word smile, such as people commonly say, "Smile and people smile with you; frown and you frown alone." Actually, there are two forms if the word smile. There is the noun representing the smile itself, and the verb form that iss the act of smiling and called the aforementioned Dushine smile. There are two substitutes for the word smile: beam and grin. For example, the boy received a bicycle for Christmas and he was beaming. Alternately, the word grin is more common, as in George has a foolish grin on his face after telling a joke.

Do all people smile? Probably not. You rarely see a farmer or industrial worker smile. Did Galileo, Plato, or Aristotle smile? We don't know and probably never will. My guess is that they did not smile very much if at all, because life was tough in those days, as a smile would certainly be regarded as a sign of weakness. Perhaps, that is true today, but I doubt it.

Girls smile a lot – or should I say women. Clearly, it seems as though they would wish people to like them.

Now, here is an interesting case. Some speakers in TV in the modern world smile between sentences. It works. They are in fact more effective than those who do not. Also, smiles sell toothpaste.

Can a smile be a sign of aggression? Yes, and no. Usually not. A smile is usually a sign of friendship. But in gangster and western movie, a toothy smile is a sign of, "I don't like you." Do football coaches on the sidelines smile? I wonder.

Lately, people have been wearing face masks to protect against a COVID virus. Can you detect a smile behind the mask? Some people say they can, you can always rely on the twinkle of an eye. Here is a smiley story. I was walking down the hallway at the university and came upon a student basketball player. Being behind the times in that regard, I asked him what a point guard was. He smiled with a big grin and told me. We came upon some other students and they were also smiling as big as life. The traditional roles of teacher-student were reversed. Now that is a real reason to smile.

My goal is to make someone happy every day. So I'm going to finish now and find someone to smile at.

Author: Harry Katzan, Jr.

The Window

Now why would anyone write about one of the most common things in the modern world: a window. After all, there are windows all over the place, and many of them don't have anything covering them up. Probably, there is an interest in windows – especially open ones – because there is almost always a sort of mystery associated with a window. There is natural inclination to find out what's going on. Is it something new and challenging, is it something drastic, is it something that is exceedingly happy or terribly sad?

Try to conceptualize strolling in the country side and coming upon an older building with blown out open windows, what is the first thing you think? Probably it is that no one cares. But that is not necessarily true. Perhaps the owner has passed away and just does not know that the beloved structure with damaged windows is in need of repair. Does caring end with death? Well, that is an open item. It seems that life in the modern world is nothing more than an ever expanding set of open items. Back to the wide world of windows.

It is entirely possible that there were never any covers of any kind over the rectangular "holes in a proverbial wall". The place was simply not finished, a commonplace consequence for a variety of everyday reasons. What about the windows in some of those middle-eastern homes. It seems as though they typically don't have anything covering the windows – at least that's how they are portrayed in the daily news. Probably it is easier to shoot through an open window and even an open door. That pertains to inside out and is likely true of outside in.

Modern office buildings are frequently designed to be window friendly and look like walls of glass. Obviously there are supporting structures placed in strategic locations to keep the whole thing up. They are certainly hot in summer and cold in winter giving a lot of work for heating and air conditioning people and also window washers, in addition to window covers and stuff like that.

A thing that some people apparently do is look into other people's windows to see what is going on. The first assumption made in this case is that the objective is to look at the people in hope of seeing something juicy. But how juicy can it really be? Probably, the objective for a good number of inside lookers – called peeping toms – is simply to see how the decorations look. Illegal activity is another thing that is too complicated for words.

Now looking out of a window could also be pretty interesting since windows are up a bit and a person can see farther out. So that brings up an unusual question. Why don't artistic painters depict scenes from a raised position? Of course, some do but not many. Practically everything that one could think of has been done – somewhere in the vast world – even painting a window scape.

There are additional sorts of windows, many of them. What about the windows associated with computers. An electronic display device is used for input and output on most modern computers, as well as tablets and smart phones. In fact, it is common to see windows inside of windows, and so forth. Millions of dollars are regularly spent by electrical engineers designing display technology enabling windows to be brighter and more readable. Practically everyone knows these days that a piece of software called an operating system is needed to use a computer and that includes phones and tablets, including music players and games. There is a major one called Windows produced by the Microsoft Corporation and the name is trademarked.

Motor vehicles have windows to see out of. The main window is called the windshield that also blocks the wind when moving. Some early cars and trucks did not have wind shields and the driver and front passenger had to wear goggles, much like airplane pilots. In vehicles, there are also side windows, a rear window, and a top window sometimes referred to as a sun roof or a moon roof. Usually the top roof opens for added pleasure. Lately, it has become common to have the top roof cover the entire roof. It is called a panoramic roof. Here is an amazing observation. It is commonplace, especially in Florida and California, to see people riding along the motor ways with the top down. Do you remember seeing someone riding along with the sun roof open?

Have you been downtown lately? Maybe not, but major retail stores have splashy windows, usually around holidays. The main idea is to put people into the holiday mood so they come and buy stuff that they probably do not need to buy, at least at the moment. It seems as though, however, that it is a bit more than that. It's a competition. Which store has the best windows? In this instance, it is not the window, per se, but what is displayed behind the window. Typically, the store will feature the pleasing and esthetically appropriate items to showcase. There are even businesses that will prepare windows for a fee, but the pleasure is often in the doing in addition to the result.

Have you ever ridden in an airplane? If you have, then you can guess what this paragraph is going to be all about. If you're lucky, you had the experience of flying in a private jet. Most people say it is pure pleasure. But why? You will soon find out. In the past, commercial air travel was a pleasure. You checked your luggage at the curb and proceeded forthwith to check in at the counter. The passenger space was ample and a meal was usually served if flight time permitted it. If you were fortunate enough to travel first class, you enjoyed orange juice or champagne when you got to your seat that was also first class. During flight, it used to be interesting to look out to see what is going on, and the seats and windows were aligned to facilitate this form of activity. Well, those days are long gone. In order to maximize revenue, airlines have stuffed many seats into a space that was limited to start with, so that a real window is unlikely. Airplane builders have come up with a new kind of window; a window that is not a window, but a computer screen showing an outside scene. The seats and windows are still not aligned, but passengers do not care after they go through check in.

Welcome to "Windows of the World". You've undoubtedly seen a sign like that, somewhere in this vast country. As mentioned, if you can think it, then it probably exists. Scenic attractions commonly view their services as a window to something fun, enjoyable, and worthy of your attention. A good book is a window to whatever the book contains. Hundreds of "Windows to ..." can easily be imagined.

An interval of time can also be regarded as a window, as in "You have a time window of three days to get to the west coast". Almost anything that is time dependent can be expressed in terms of a window. Moreover, anything you can see through is a window, even though it may be on the floor or the ceiling. Most windows are rectangular, although some are round, square, and all flavors of shape.

So just what is the window and just what is the something else. A window has been defined as an opening in a wall to allow light, air, or just about anything else to get in. If you break a hole in the side of a barn that allows in light, air, dust, and all manners of bugs, have you created a window? Most people would class that as a nasty hole in the wall. Not a window. Many people say that anything you can see through is a window, even though it may be on the floor or the ceiling. Most windows are rectangular, although some are round, square, and all flavors of shape. To finish the definition of a window, it is an opening with casements or sashes that contain transparent material, such as glass or plastic, capable of being open or closed. A glass window that can't be opened and an opaque windows are still windows. Some windows are classed by what they do for people. But a window, per se, does not really do anything. It just sits there, looking kind of stupid. A ticket window is used to distribute tickets, so to speak, to customers who use the same facility to obtain them. But, isn't that exactly what most things in the world do. They kind of sit there looking kind of stupid for other people to use.

It's getting a little cool in here so I'll close the window.

Author: Harry Katzan, Jr.

END OF THE AFTERWORD

About This Book

This is a book of fiction and is intended for the entertainment of the reader. The Iranian students are real, although their actual lives are not known.

The reference to Bill Donovan is true. He is the attorney that negotiated for the release of Gary Powers. He did become the President of a well-known university in Brooklyn, New York.

All references to aircraft, pilots, and procedures are all made up for the occasion. Some references may be true or correct, as the case may be, but only by accident.

The reference to drones that carry people is only an extension of the idea of a space ship.

It is possible that a planet out in space somewhere is identical with that of planet Earth. There are billions if not more, planets in the universe, so who knows.

It was a distinct pleasure to write about Matt, Ashley, Anna, the General, and the Sir Charles Bunday. They are foremost in my imagination.

My wife Margaret and our daughter Kathy helped me whenever necessary and did so with great pleasure.

Thanks for reading the book. The book follows the usual procedure of no violence, no sex, and no bad language. It is accessible to readers of all ages.

About the Author

Harry Katzan, Jr. is a professor who has written several books and many papers on computers and service, in addition to some novels. He has been a advisor to the executive board of a major bank and a general consultant on various disciplines. He and his wife have lived in Switzerland where he was a banking consultant and a visiting professor. He is an avid runner and has completed 94 marathons including Boston 13 times and New York 14 times. He holds bachelors, masters, and doctorate degrees.

Books by Harry Katzan, Jr.

COMPUTERS AND INFORMATION SYSTEMS

Advanced Programming
APL Programming and Computer Techniques
APL Users Guide
Computer Organization and the System/370
A PL/I Approach to Programming Languages
Introduction to Programming Languages
Operating Systems
Information Technology
Computer Data Security
Introduction to Computer Science
Computer Systems Organization and Programming
Computer Data Management and Database Technology
Systems Design and Documentation
Microprogramming Primer
The IBM 5100 Portable Computer
Fortran 77
The Standard Data Encryption Algorithm
Introduction to Distributed Data Processing
Distributed Information Systems
Invitation to Pascal
Invitation to Forth
Microcomputer Graphics and Programming Techniques
Invitation to Ada
Invitation to Ada and Ada Reference Manual
Invitation to Mapper
Operating Systems (2nd Edition)
Local Area Networks
Invitation to MVS (with D. Tharayil)
Privacy, Identity, and Cloud Computing

BUSINESS AND MANAGEMENT

Multinational Computer Systems
Office Automation
Management Support Systems
A Manager's Guide to Productivity, Quality
Circles, and Industrial Robots
Quality Circle Management
Service and Advanced Technology

RESEARCH

Managing Uncertainty

SERVICE SCIENCE

A Manager's Guide to Service Science
Foundations of Service Science
Service Science
Introduction to Service
Service Concepts for Management
A Collection of Service Essays
Hospitality and Service

NOVELS

The Mysterious Case of the Royal Baby
The Curious Case of the Royal Marriage
The Auspicious Case of the General and the Royal Family
A Case of Espionage
Shelter in Place
The Virus
The Pandemic

Life is Good
The Vaccine
A Tale of Discovery
The Terrorist Plot
An Untimely Situation
The Final Escape

LITTLE BOOK SERIES

The Little Book of Artificial Intelligence
The Little Book of Service Management
The Little Book of Cybersecurity
The Little Book of Cloud Computing

END OF BOOKS BY HARRY KATZAN JR.

**End of the Book
The Final Escape**

**And the Book
The Stage Play of The
Final Escape**

Printed in the United States
by Baker & Taylor Publisher Services